D1569176

PERIL IN PARADISE

A Mango Bay Mystery

PERIL IN PARADISE

•

Marty Ambrose

AVALON BOOKS
NEW YORK

Published by Thomas Bouregy & Co., Inc.
160 Madison Avenue, New York, NY 10016

Library of Congress Cataloging-in-Publication Data

Ambrose, Marty.
  Peril in paradise / Marty Ambrose.
       p. cm.
    ISBN 978-0-8034-9939-3 (hard cover : acid-free paper)
  1. Journalists—Fiction.   2. Women detectives—Fiction.
3. Murder—Fiction.   4. Florida—Fiction.   I. Title.

PS3601.M368P47 2009
813'.6—dc22

                                          2008031628

PRINTED IN THE UNITED STATES OF AMERICA
ON ACID-FREE PAPER
BY HADDON CRAFTSMEN, BLOOMSBURG, PENNSYLVANIA

I would like to thank my husband, Jim, who has been my editor for many years. Also, many thanks to my mother's keen eye for proofreading; she never misses a mistake in any manuscript. They are my biggest fan club—along with my beautiful sister, Elizabeth.

My gratitude also goes out to my dear friend and editing partner of more than a decade, Tina Wainscott, who never loses the faith.

And last but not least, I'd like to acknowledge my agent and constant cheerleader, Roberta Brown. You're simply the best!

"The only true paradises are the paradises which we have lost."

Marcel Proust

Chapter One

The first time I saw Jack Hillman he was bare-chested.

I hadn't wanted to look, but it was like passing a particularly horrendous accident on the road: I couldn't resist a peek. There he was, sitting on his second-floor redwood deck with the sunlight glinting off the rolls of flesh that hung around his middle. Yikes.

At one time, his physique might've been impressive, but now gravity had done its thing and his skin was sagging with a lumpy softness reserved for mattresses left in the rain. To paraphrase Milton, the mind might be its own place, but the body is rooted in the here and now. And Jack's had seen better days.

Granted, he wasn't posturing—just proudly bare-chested. But still, I could've done without seeing that particular wreck.

1

I'd been at the *Coral Island Observer* only one month when Anita Sanders, the editor, called me into her office, although calling the tiny, walled-off cubicle an "office" was like calling a rock a precious gem. It was, nonetheless, the closest thing our little paper had to a boss' lair. The rest of us—a part-time secretary/advertising manager and me—had to make do with two rickety desks, an outmoded Dell desktop computer, and a battered old filing cabinet in the main room.

"Mallie, I've got a story for you," Anita began in a raspy voice. She tapped her half-smoked cigarette in an ashtray, one already heaped with previously smoked Camel stubs—no wimpy filter tips ever touched her mouth. "Jack Hillman is beginning his Summer Writers' Institute, and I want you to cover it. Interview him. Attend some of the workshops. Talk to some of the writers. Give our readers some first-hand info."

"Jack does a workshop on this island?" I was amazed. He was a pretty well-known writer of true crime fiction. One had even been made into a feature film starring that guy from the *X-Files* show whose name I could never remember. Except that it ended with the same letters as *anchovy*.

"Yep. He's a longtime resident of Coral Island. Has an old house here and likes to spend the summers fishing and boating—and doing an occasional writer's institute." Anita took another long drag on her cigarette, drawing in her thin cheeks. She was painfully lean, with leathery skin from too much sun and lots of vertical lines from too many cigarettes.

"It sounds interesting."

"A lot better than all those boring bike path committee meetings you've been covering."

"I wouldn't call them boring." I'd call them-drop-dead dull. The only exciting thing that ever happened was when aging veteran, One-Eyed Al, would pop out his glass eye and toss it from hand to hand.

At my lie, Anita gave a short bark of laughter that turned into a smoker's cough. "Look, so far your work hasn't stunk, but I want to break you of that college essay style you seem to love. Maybe giving you a story with a little more meat to it will help. You've gotta grab the reader, but keep it tight and simple."

I was silent. I needed the job too much to argue with her—or point out offices were supposed to be "smoke-free" environments. Besides, she was probably right. Cranking out newspaper stories was a struggle for me because I had no experience with that type of writing. My most recent day job as a substitute high school teacher in Orlando hadn't prepared me for much of anything except how to scribble hall passes and make sure senior girls didn't sneak into the bathroom to dye their hair green with paint stolen from art class. My night job at Disney World left me with even fewer verbal skills, unless you consider the ability to sing "It's a Small World" in five different languages a skill.

"I've already called Hillman—he's expecting you at his house." She ground out her cigarette in a nearby ashtray.

"Where's that?" I reached into my large canvas bag and fished out my little spiral-bound official reporter's notepad that made me at least look like a real journalist.

"He lives south of Mango Bay on a part of the island called The Mounds. It's off Seashell Lane. The houses are built right into the side of some ancient shell mounds—his is the two-story."

I was jotting down all of this in my notepad as fast as I could.

"Just to warn you, kiddo, Jack can be a bit . . . eccentric. Don't take him too seriously. He was a security guard at the Coca-Cola factory in town before he became a big-name writer." She lit up another cigarette. "Now he likes to pretend he's Hemingway or something."

"I'll try not to be too intimidated." Irony threaded through my voice.

Anita raised gray brows as she handed me a copy of his last book, *Men on Death Row*. His picture was on the back cover. Barrel-chested with a full head of graying hair, he had the look of a man whose best years had passed him by like a flock of birds gone south. But he was still stubbornly entrenched in the nest of midlife, unwilling to admit that his season had come and gone.

"I look forward to meeting him." *I might skip reading the book, though.* True crime wasn't my thing. After perusing his first book, *Night Games*, years ago I decided macho-gritty confessions weren't for me. And men on death row were even less my thing.

"Good." She turned toward her computer screen in an obvious dismissal.

I exited her smoke-filled cubicle and went to my desk to pick up an extra official reporter's notepad— just in case the interviews grew lengthy. I dropped it in my canvas bag and it was immediately swallowed up by the jumble of pens, keys, wallet, lipstick, checkbook, sunblock, mini-mouthwash, and various other assorted daily necessities. I liked to carry a little chaos with me—it made life interesting.

"I heard you were doing a story on Jack Hillman," Sandy, the advertising manager/secretary, commented. She had long, straight brown hair, wore round glasses and, from what I could tell in my short time at the paper, was on a perpetual search for the holy grail of diets in between badgering local businesses to buy advertising space in the paper.

"Boy, news travels fast in an eight-hundred-square-foot office."

"Anita e-mailed me about the story." She pointed a pudgy finger at the small Dell computer screen.

Something hanging from her sleeve caught my eye. "What's that?"

"Oh, this? It's a sales ticket." She tucked the tag back into her sleeve. "I haven't decided whether I want to keep the dress or not. I might need a smaller size soon."

"Good strategy." The red knit dress was already so tight, she practically burst out of the seams.

"Watch out for Jack—he's a real lady killer," Sandy warned in a light tone.

"What do you mean?"

She shrugged. "He's got quite a reputation on the island for . . . well, hitting on everything in a skirt and stealing women that aren't his. You know, other men's wives and that kind of thing. He's technically single now, but he's never without some young blond."

"So he likes blonds?"

She nodded.

"Then I guess I'm in the clear." I patted my wild red curls with a smile. My hair was my one vanity. It was a vibrant scarlet color—not auburn or russet—but a deep fire-engine red that always drew stares and questions about whether it was my natural color or not. The rest of my appearance was sort of bland—blue eyes, lots of freckles, and a figure that could only be called skinny. I had that girl-next-door look that rarely drew a second look. Except for my hair—it drew a second and sometimes even a third look.

"You're as safe as a bug in a rug," Sandy agreed, but her glance lingered on my hair.

"Thanks," I said dryly.

"Oh, and don't forget Anita needs the first draft of your bike path story update tomorrow morning. She'll want to do her usual slash and trash editing by the Friday deadline."

I winced. "It's pretty much the same story as last week. Salty Bob won't give up his easement, and everybody on the committee is totally fed up with him. They actually talked about condemning the easement and then taking over his property without his permission."

Sandy was shaking her head. "That's not going to work. They need to try to connect with his inner child. Find out why he's such a jerk. It's all right here in *O*." She held up a copy of Oprah Winfrey's magazine. "People act hostile because they have unresolved conflicts from their childhoods. Maybe Bob was ignored."

"Maybe." Along with her diets, Sandy spent an inordinately large amount of time reading self-help books, self-improvement magazines, and self-fulfillment pamphlets. But, then again, she might have a point about Salty Bob. He could've been an ignored middle child. Could explain why he was so doggoned stubborn about getting his way with that easement.

As I left the newspaper office located in a tiny strip mall at the island center, I thought about Sandy's self-help quest. Maybe it wasn't such a bad thing. If I'd planned better, thought more clearly about what I wanted in my life, I wouldn't be in my late twenties at a weekly newspaper on a rural island in Southwest Florida. But what else could I do with a BA in comparative literature, a string of unsuccessful jobs, and no man on the horizon since my last boyfriend left for Arizona to "find himself"?

I was lucky to have the job at the *Observer*—courtesy

of my great aunt Lily—the grand dame of Coral Island and my favorite relative. She and I were *simpatico*, which meant she didn't call me "Mixed-up Mallie" like the rest of my family, and she didn't criticize me for the lack of "direction" in my life. I preferred to think of my lifestyle as a quest for adventure. I liked it better not knowing what would come around the next corner, rather than have my whole life planned out like a roadmap of boring ruts and routines.

I climbed into my ancient Ford truck and cranked up the engine. "Come on, Rusty, do your thing." I pressed the pedal down a few times in rapid succession. The engine sputtered, then turned over. Quickly, I threw it into gear and rolled down the window to catch a little of the early morning breeze. Almost June, the suffocating Florida heat hadn't blanketed the island yet, but it was coming. I reached into my glove compartment and pulled out a bottle of Hawaiian Tropic Sunblock with an SPF of fifteen and an overpowering smell of sickly sweet coconut. Slathering it on liberally, I checked my peeling, red nose in the rearview mirror. It was still mildly sunburned. Much as I loved my red hair, the pale, freckled skin that went with it was less than compatible with the scorching Florida sun.

Maneuvering Rusty onto Cypress Road, which was the main drag of Coral Island, I took in a deep cleansing breath of sea air and tried to appreciate my surroundings. This swampy, coastal island, touted as a "lush, tropical paradise" in the marketing advertisements that appeared in the *Observer* was, in reality, a hot, humid, and buggy spit of land only twenty miles long and about a mile wide. Tucked inside a ring of barrier islands, it boasted no fabulous stretches of sandy beaches or high-rise hotels. Just good fishing. Still, it had its charm. A small dune that passed for a beach was located on the northern tip on Mango Bay, and bountiful vegetation was everywhere, including tall, thin pines and clusters of seagrape.

I eased up on the accelerator and made a left turn on Seashell Lane. The unpaved, sandy road curved around dense foliage and gumbo limbo trees only to end at the tiny settlement high atop thirty-foot shell mounds. Spectacular, they rose up from the shoreline of Coral Island Sound in giant white formations, with a grove of exotic trees set beyond the highest point. Two houses were perched about halfway up the mounds—one a long, flat stuccoed dwelling with a wraparound screened porch, and the other, a two-storied white clap-board structure, complete with dormer windows and a small, open-air second-floor deck.

That's when I saw Jack. He was lounging on a white Adirondack chair on the deck, soaking up some morning sunlight, half-naked, with a drink in his hand. *Jeez.*

As if sensing my scrutiny, he glanced down and met my stare. Unembarrassed, he simply waved and turned his face toward the sun again.

I blinked a couple of times, trying to clear the image out of my mind, but it perversely refused to leave. It would be a long time before I was able to forget that I'd seen that sagging ruin of a man's body.

Turning my truck into the driveway, I noticed several cars already parked there—presumably the participants of the Writers' Institute. It was an interesting array of makes and models. A large, old model Cadillac with New Mexico license plates; a Ford escort, complete with hatchback and chipped paint along the sides; and a small, snappy Miata convertible. A silver Dodge Viper was also parked next to the house. A shiny testament to testosterone, it bore a license plate that read, "Author." Presumably, it was Hillman's vehicle.

I liked to match people to their cars, knowing that my battered, old Ford truck spoke volumes about my own lifestyle: little disposable income but a lot of heart. Oh, yeah, a mirror reflection of me.

Turning off the engine, I climbed out of my truck and made for the winding stone path that cut through the thick, overgrown bougainvillea bushes. A couple of long, spindly branches stuck out and thorns brushed against my legs. Grateful I was wearing a pair of old jeans, I kept moving until I reached a clearing. A small screened porch jutted out from the front of the house, a small, brass captain's bell—like the kind on a boat— was near the door. I gave the cord a quick pull. The bell clanged and a young woman instantly appeared.

"Hi." She pushed open the screen door. "I'm Chrissy Anders."

I immediately noted her long, honey-blond hair and

shapely figure highlighted by cutoffs and a tight T-shirt with "Save the Earth" splashed across the front in gold letters. Her face and body had that perfectly toned and tanned look of someone who spent a lot of time outdoors hiking and kayaking and jogging and all that kind of stuff that created a disgustingly healthy glow. At least, I told myself that. It made accepting my own freckles, blotchy skin, and thin form a little easier to take.

"I'm Mallie Monroe, a reporter with the *Observer*." I started to shake hands with her when Hillman appeared behind her—now wearing a pair of shorts in olive drab and a matching short-sleeved shirt. Quite an improvement, really.

"Jack Hillman. How ya doin?" He pumped my hand in a strong grip. "Anita told me you'd be attending the Writer's Institute. We're glad to have you. Very glad." His glance had settled on my hair.

"I'm not exactly an attendee. I work for the newspaper, and I'm here to do a story on the Institute—"

"That's even better. You can learn some pointers on how to write a nonfiction article. I worked on several newspapers before I became a fiction writer, and I can show you how to knock off a front-page, potential Pulitzer Prize–winning story in less than an hour."

"But . . ."

"It'll get old bullheaded Anita off your back. I pledge, promise, and promote success." His florid face broke into a wide smile that even I had to admit was sort of appealing in an aging, bad-boy kind of way. And the prospect of getting Anita off my back was even more so.

"But the story has to be about the Writers' Institute," I said weakly, knowing I was caving in, if for no other reason than Hillman's persuasive use of alliteration.

"Sure. Sure. Everyone is already in the Florida room. Let's go on in so you can meet them." He led me into the house and through a very modern, very gourmet kitchen, complete with granite countertops, an elaborate gas stove, and a pot rack with the latest shiny red cookware. I took a sidelong glance at his protruding middle. It was obvious he liked to eat, but now I knew he liked to cook. Interesting.

I strolled into the expansive Florida room and was again treated to a room decorated with affluence and good taste. Jalousie windows surrounded the room on three sides, and wood floors gleamed beneath my sandals. Wicker furniture upholstered with tropical print cushions was scattered around the room, along with a mahogany antique or two. Hardly the kind of room I expected from a man who prided himself on his gritty writing prowess but, the more I saw of his house, the more I began to see Jack had intriguing dimensions. Not the least of which was he could lounge half-naked on his deck with this many people in the house.

"Hello, I'm Burt Morris and this is my wife, Betty," a tall, middle-aged man said from the small bar area off to the side of the room. Betty was equally as tall, with a wide mouth and large teeth. Both of them, in fact, had a vaguely equine appearance. "We're from Tucumcari, New Mexico, and we're writing a series of short stories about the Old West." He held up a pitcher. "Care for a margarita?"

"No, thanks."

"Suit yourself." He poured the pale green liquid into two large frosted glasses and handed one to Betty.

"And you've already met Chrissy," Hillman interjected, his arm snaking around the blond's waist.

"I'm writing eco-conscious poetry. You know, like Thoreau. A lot of people don't realize he wrote verse, but he did, and it was great stuff. Jack said the best way to break in is through an environmental poetry blog with lots of my own poems." She gave a satisfied smile. "Isn't that way cool?"

"Totally." I was sort of impressed. It sounded plausible.

"I'm George B . . . B . . . Barret," a young man standing off by himself stammered. Thin and wiry, he had long hair that partially obscured the upper section of his face. The lower half was covered by his slender hand, thus making it difficult to hear him very well. He mumbled something else that I couldn't quite make out.

"Georgy here is working on a nonfiction book on overcoming shyness," Hillman said. He strolled over to George and thumped him on the back a couple of times. "Yessiree. He's going to be putting out the next best-seller."

Okay.

George coughed each time Hillman slapped him between the shoulders, but managed a small nod in between hacks.

"And that's our little group," Hillman continued.

"What about you, Mallie? What are you working on?" Chrissy asked.

All eyes riveted on me. "I . . . uh . . . I'm not working on anything as ambitious as the rest of you. I just started a new job as a journalist and I'm trying to learn how to write better news stories."

"There are no little goals," Burt spoke up and everyone else joined in to chant the last half: "Only little writers."

Hillman clapped his hands. "Good work everybody. We'll teach Mary how to motivate herself."

"It's Mallie."

"Oh . . . sorry, Milly."

Close enough.

The Institute might not be large, but what they lacked in numbers they made up for in enthusiasm, and Jack was like the benign, genial *pater familias*. Maybe this whole thing wouldn't be so bad after all.

Hillman motioned everyone over to a large oval table, and it seemed as if the mood instantly changed like an atmospheric shift before a sudden, violent storm. My fellow writers settled into their seats, and I followed suit, setting my hundred pound canvas bag on the floor.

"Now, since Milly is new to our group, let's start with a recent story her editor sent over." He passed out copies of last week's *Observer.* "This is one of her latest articles on the bike path. It's typical of a small-town paper, but there's still room for improvement, don't you think?"

Everyone nodded.

Uh-oh.

I suddenly had this feeling of being back in third grade when my mother grilled me over making a "B" in English grammar. I loved literature but hated nitpicking sentences apart. She had waved the report card around, demanding to know why I was letting my whole future slip away because I couldn't seem to conjugate irregular verbs. Of course, the real culprit today was my hardnosed editor. *Damn her anyway!*

Hillman picked up a yellow highlighter. "Let's go through the article paragraph by paragraph." He sliced the marker across the title as if wielding a knife. "Look at the title: 'Bike Path Decision in Flux'." He laughed. "How can a path be in flux? That's a hackneyed phrase if I've ever heard one. It's like something you'd expect a high school journalism student to come up with." All of the other writers dutifully whipped out highlighter pens and repeated his motion on their copies of the *Observer.*

And that was just the beginning. He tore into every paragraph with fiendish delight, chopping and slicing at my every word until there was nothing left except a few bits and pieces of sentences that somehow survived, gasping for life.

I was in a state of shock. My mouth had turned to cotton, and my heart thumped in my chest like a hammer hitting an anvil. Where had that genial, albeit half-naked, host gone? He had somehow turned into a fault-finding, vicious critic of the worst kind—just like my mother. All of a sudden, I regretted not having taken Burt and Betty up on their offer of a margarita.

As I glanced around the table, no one looked up. Not one pair of eyes met mine to offer even a glimpse of sympathy. I felt like roadkill on the highway to news writing paradise.

And then I found out why the group had turned mute to my plight. I was the first person in the hot seat that morning. Each took turns as the recipient of Hillman's verbal assault—even Chrissy. One by one, we submitted ourselves to cruel jabs, mean taunts, and nasty ridicule. And no one left the room—except for Betty. She took a short hiatus, probably for a straight shot of tequila, but returned within ten minutes still able to walk.

The critiquing went on for most of the day—with only a brief break for lunch. I could only presume that this was business as usual at the Institute, and everyone thought learning by humiliation the best way to become a successful writer.

Jack appeared to relish his role as a hard-nosed writing teacher, letting each of us have it on the chin with both fists. I spent much of the time fantasizing about slamming him back with my own knuckle sandwich of literary criticism. Small comfort.

It was early afternoon before we broke up, and I could only hope my all-day, roll-on deodorant lived up to its promise. I'd moved way beyond the cold sweat stage.

"That about does it for today." He slapped both of his heavy thighs. "Do your editing work tonight and then bring back what you have for tomorrow's session—especially you, Chrissy. That last poem on global warming really sucked." He rose from his chair, stretched his arms overhead, and exhaled in a long sigh of contentment. "I'm going for a quick dip in the hot tub. Anyone care to join me?"

George shook his head, followed by Betty and Burt.

"Maybe later," Chrissy managed between trembling lips. A tear slid down the side of her heart-shaped face, but she brushed it away with a quick swipe of her hand.

"Okay. Later, dudes and dudettes." Hillman swaggered off, actually whistling a little tune under his breath.

Chrissy let out a sob and ran from the table, leaving the rest of us, sitting there, stunned.

"Does this happen every day?" I finally found my voice.

"P . . . P . . . P . . . pretty much," George closed his eyes briefly and sighed.

Burt held up his third margarita. "Betty and I fortify ourselves. It's the only way we make it through these daily sessions."

"But why subject yourself to this kind of torture?" I asked, amazed.

"We want to b...b...become b...b...better writers," George said. He covered his mouth with his hand and added something else that I couldn't make out. But I thought I heard him murmur Chrissy's name.

"I'm surprised someone hasn't wrung his neck before this. Or at least told him off." I was getting my wits about me again.

Betty and Burt just took another swig of their margaritas. George shook his head.

"I, for one, have had enough of Hillman's kind of help, thank you very much." I grabbed my bag and my last shreds of self-respect and left the table.

I'd stomped halfway to my truck when I remembered that I still had to interview Hillman for my article on the Writers' Institute. Groaning, I went around to the back of the house and spied Hillman sitting in the hot tub, drink in one hand and neon pink cell phone in the other. When he saw me, he started slightly and ended the call. Then, he turned his attention toward me. "What can I do ya for, Milly? Care to join me?" His eyes fastened on my hair. He ran his tongue across thick lips.

"No, thanks." I swallowed hard. He was bare-chested again. *Yuck.* "I need to do a brief interview with you about the Institute—for my article."

"Sure. Love to." He took a long swallow of his drink. "You can bring in the finished version for an editing session later this week."

Fat chance.

"Come back in a couple of hours and I'll be ready for you." The cell phone rang and he waved me off.

Grateful to get away before another proposition, I hopped in my truck and drove off just as Chrissy was coming out in a skimpy bright yellow-flowered bikini. Her shoulders were squared and her mouth drawn in a thin line. She'd probably turned angry by now. Good. I hope she really gives it to him, I muttered to myself as I revved away. As I looked back, I shivered in spite of the heat. Jack wasn't conducting writers' workshops—it was more like a little shop of horrors. And I wouldn't be back—except to get my interview.

I drove to the main road and made my way to Mango Bay—the largest town on Coral Island, located on the north tip. Although calling the smattering of buildings a town could be construed as gross exaggeration, Mango Bay nonetheless functioned as the hub of the island.

It included a small clapboard general store called Whiteside's, which had been there since the home-steading days on the island at the beginning of the century. Slightly bigger than a Circle K, the store included a post office in back, dry-cleaning pick-up at the counter, and various tourist items like shell-encrusted ashtrays and bright green rubber alligators. Aside from Whiteside's, the tiny island village also boasted a small art gallery, a bait shack, and a seafood restaurant— Capt'n Harry's. Mostly retirees and fishermen lived at Mango Bay but, since it overlooked a picturesque view of the water, some larger homes had recently sprung up between the trailers and fishing shacks. I was temporarily staying at the Twin Palms RV Resort—the trailer park right on the point, and the only place on the island with a small beach.

The main attraction for me right now was Capt'n Harry's—a rustic restaurant decorated on the outside with old fishing nets and yellowed buoys. Dismal nautical décor aside, it faced the water and served the best crab cakes I'd ever eaten. I ordered the seafood basket, which I took outside to the long, wooden dock that stretched out into the bay. I sat for an hour or two, watching the pelicans and trying to figure out how I was going to tell Anita I wouldn't be attending the Writers' Institute. I didn't want to jeopardize my job, but I couldn't go back there and let Hillman rip me up and down simply because he got some twisted thrill from seeing people squirm.

I had enough of that in my life. As the youngest child, I'd been endlessly compared to my brother, a corporate attorney, and my sister, a top-notch design engineer. Not only was I not a top-notch anything, I couldn't seem to settle into any profession longer than a year or two. In between jobs, I'd substitute teach and hook up with boyfriends who liked the same carefree, gypsy lifestyle. I had my truck and my antique Airstream trailer and, when things got dull, I'd just pick up and move to another city. I'd started out in St. Louis, Missouri, where I was born, and kept moving south. I never got bored, and I never got stuck in a rut. But I never felt like I belonged anywhere either.

A huge brown pelican wheeled overhead and then dropped down in sudden descent to scoop up an unsuspecting fish. I'd just have to tell Anita the truth. I'd do the article about the Writers' Institute, but I wouldn't attend any more of the workshops. One was plenty. Old hatchet-face's criticism of my articles would have to be enough.

As I rose to my feet, the seabreeze lifted the curls off the back of my neck. I turned my face to the water and closed my eyes. For a few moments, that habitual burning restlessness inside me settled, and I felt a moment of peace.

A pair of seagulls squawked in a loud, mocking cackle. My eyes snapped open, and the moment vanished like a dream in the dawn. Okay, so maybe this wasn't exactly paradise, but at least I wasn't in Orlando substitute teaching by day and taking tickets at the entrance to Magic Kingdom by night.

I checked my Mickey Mouse watch (courtesy of my tenure at Disney World). Almost seven-thirty. I'd do the interview, edit my bike path story for tomorrow, and call Anita to break the bad news to her that I was officially a Writers' Institute dropout.

I climbed into my truck and drove back to Hillman's house on the shell mounds. With evening drawing near, the sky exploded off to the west in vivid shades, ranging from soft rose to a crimson stripe of color near the horizon. It splayed across the sky like a blood-red gash of color before the darkness set in. All of a sudden, I shivered and turned away.

Parking my truck, I noticed all the cars were gone except the Viper.

I clanged the captain's bell on the front porch. No one answered. I knocked on the screen door. Still no answer. "Mr. Hillman?" I called out, peering through the screen.

He didn't appear. It was quiet, deadly quiet. No droning of a television, no music, nothing—except the steady hum of evening crickets. I pushed the screen door open and stepped inside. "Mr. Hillman?"

I walked through the house and into the Florida room, my footsteps falling on the wood floor with a soft clump. Eyeing the table where we had sat earlier for our individual assassinations, I shuddered. It was empty, but the memories of this morning lingered.

Maybe Hillman had forgotten that he'd agreed to do an interview with me and gone out. But then again, his car was still in the driveway.

Looking out the widows of the Florida room, I checked the hot tub. Nope, not there either. I placed my hands on my hips and sighed. Where the heck was he? I *had* to do this interview.

I passed through the kitchen and glanced down a wide hallway at a home office, separated from the rest of the house by curtained French doors. One door stood open, and I could make out floor to ceiling bookshelves. Slowly, I approached the open door, warning bells going off in my mind. Something was wrong, really wrong.

Hesitantly, I peered around the door. Sheer, black fright swept through me. I must've screamed, but I'm not exactly sure what sound came out of my mouth. It might've been a shout, a scream, or a loud gurgle. All I knew was that Jack Hillman's body was flung backward in his desk chair, eyes staring blankly at the ceiling and blood seeping from the would over his heart.

He was dead.

Chapter Two

For a few long moments, I didn't move. I couldn't. I stood frozen to the spot. Then, my legs began to shake, every muscle seized by quaking tremors. My throat tightened, and my chest felt as though it would burst.

"Keep calm," I heard a voice say as if from a long distance away. It took me a second or two to realize that it was mine.

"Call nine-one-one—that's what you do in an emergency."

Maybe the paramedics could revive him.

I took another glance at Hillman. He wasn't moving. He wasn't breathing.

"Make the call. Now!"

Willing my feet to move, I stumbled out of the room and located a cordless phone in the kitchen. I made the emergency call, and within ten minutes, the medics, the police, and the firefighters all descended on Hillman's house with the force of a tropical storm. It was a blur of activity for a short while, with various men and women shouting orders at each other as sirens blared outside and cell phones rang inside. When they approached me, all I could do was point my shaky hand down the hall-way toward the room and Hillman's body.

A young woman with a stethoscope around her neck finally noticed my dazed state and took my arm. She led me into the Florida room and sat me down on the sofa. "Are you all right?" She took my pulse.

"I . . . I'm not sure. I've never seen a dead body be-fore. At least not a person. I've seen a couple of roadkills, but they were just small animals—and not very close up. I passed them in my truck, you know—on the road. Oh, and I had an uncle who passed away three years ago and I saw him in the casket during the funeral service, but he was . . . uh, embalmed," I babbled. I couldn't seem to stop myself. It was something I did whenever I was nervous. I kept talking and talking and talking like my brain was an engine jammed in high gear. Eventually, I ran out of steam, but not until I covered a lot of ground and a copious amount of unrelated topics.

"Your pulse is a little fast, but I'd expect that under the circumstances." Her tone was a soothing balm on my frayed nerves. "Take a couple of deep breaths and let them out slowly."

I complied, but exhaling was difficult. The air came

out in jagged fits and starts. After a couple of tries, though, it grew easier and my breathing steadied. Whew.

"That's better. Let yourself relax."

"You must deal with this kind of thing a lot," I managed between breaths. "Dead bodies—hysterical people."

"Not all that much. Most of our calls are from elderly folks who've fallen or parents whose kids have broken an arm on their brand-new bicycle." Her mouth curved upward in a kind smile.

"Is this the person who made the call?" a brusque, masculine voice cut in.

"Yes." The young woman rose to her feet. "I'll leave her in your capable hands." I detected a note of respect, and looked up in time to see an expression of admiration on her face. I transferred my gaze in curiosity.

My eyes traveled up long legs encased in black trousers, slid past a powerful set of shoulders that strained against the fabric of his white short-sleeve shirt and tie, and ended on a darkly handsome face. He towered over the other men in the room, so much so that I had to tip my head backward to look at his face.

"I'm Detective Nick Billie." He held out his hand. I just stared. Partly, I was still in shock. But the other part of me was stunned by his compelling good looks. Black hair flowed from his forehead like a crest, and smooth olive skin stretched over high cheekbones. But it was his eyes that were most mesmerizing. Obsidian deep and dark pools of shadows and hidden dreams.

"Mallie Monroe." I shook his hand, feeling the firm strength of his fingers.

"What's your connection with Jack Hillman?" he asked.

"I . . . uh, just met him today—actually this morning. I work at the *Observer*, and my editor sent me over to do a story on his Summer Writers' Institute."

"And?"

"I attended a day-long workshop and then came back to do a personal interview. That's when I found him." I swallowed hard. "Is he . . . ?"

"Dead. Yes. He appears to have received a fatal chest wound."

"Ohmygosh!"

"Was there anyone else around when you drove up?"

"I don't think so." My neck was starting to stiffen from tilting my head backward. "Would you mind sitting down please? I'm getting a crick in my neck."

He hauled a wicker chair over and sat down.

"Thanks." *Sort of.* Even seated, Nick Billie was no less commanding. "When I arrived, the house was empty—except for Mr. Hillman."

"What time was that?"

"About half an hour ago, I think." *Why was he asking me so many questions with a suspicious tone?* Caution flared inside of me.

"And where were you before you drove back here?"

"At Capt'n Harry's. I had the seafood basket with french fries and ketchup."

His dark brows flickered a little. "Just answer the questions that I ask you please, Ms. Monroe."

"Sure. Sorry. This is my first murder." Keep the motor mouth under control, I reminded myself. He doesn't need all the details.

"So aside from this morning, you've never met Mr. Hillman before?"

"No, but I did read his first book, *Night Games.* It was really good—the kind of true crime thriller that keeps you on the edge of your seat. It wasn't too blood and guts like his latest stuff, which I've avoided. Have you read *Men on Death Row*?"

He shook his head. "I don't have time to read. I deal with real life, and real-life murders aren't all that thrilling. Mostly, they're messy and unpleasant." He rubbed the back of his neck with a weary hand.

I thought of Jack's body in the room down the hall and shuddered. "I get your point."

"Was there anything odd about the workshop this morning?"

I hesitated. "What do you mean?"

"Did anyone make threatening comments or gestures toward Mr. Hillman?"

"A few people were a little . . . upset at some of the criticism Mr. Hillman directed at them."

"Including you?"

"I guess so."

"Yes or no?"

"Yes." I looked down and picked at the dry cuticle

around my thumb. I had that uneasy feeling that arose inside when I noticed a police car in my rear view mirror on the highway. I'd let up on the gas pedal even if I weren't speeding and drive very, very carefully, anxious that maybe I had done something illegal that I wasn't aware of.

"Were you angry enough to want to hurt Mr. Hillman?"

"Not really." I kept at the thumb.

"Did you come back here to injure him?"

"No." My head snapped up at that one. "I was ticked off when he criticized my story on the bike path, but everyone else was just as upset when he tore into their work. And just because I was angry doesn't mean that I wanted to *kill* him."

For a long moment, he studied me with a speculative squint. My chin turned up in defiance. I hadn't done anything wrong. I sure as heck hadn't harmed Hillman, so why was I feeling guilty? I might have fantasized about using him for bait at the next tarpon fishing tournament, but I wouldn't have really done anything like that.

"Am I a suspect or not?" I finally summoned the nerve to ask.

"In theory, yes. You found the body. You had ample opportunity to come back here and kill Hillman. And by your own admission, he made you angry earlier today." He leaned back in the wicker chair and folded his arms across his chest. "But my gut instinct tells me you're not a killer."

"That's comforting—I guess."

For the first time his mouth turned up on one side in a lopsided smile. "That doesn't mean you're off the hook, Ms. Monroe. My gut's been wrong a time or two."

Peachy. Just peachy. I've got a cop on the case with a malfunctioning gut.

"Come to the police station tomorrow morning at the island center and we'll take your statement."

"I'm still technically a suspect?" That uneasy feeling amped up a notch.

He rose to his feet. "Don't leave the island."

"Not even to the mainland?"

He frowned at me from his considerable height. "I meant don't leave the area. We might need you for further questioning."

"My job is here—I have no intention of leaving," I reminded him. Nevertheless, images of hooking my Airstream trailer to Rusty flashed through my mind. Freedom. No ties—just open road. And no murder hanging over my head. So tempting . . .

As if divining my thoughts, Detective Billie repeated, "Stay put for awhile."

The open road fantasy faded. "Okay."

He strode out of the room and I sat there for a few minutes taking stock of my situation. It didn't look good.

The frenzied activity in the house had settled down, with only a few people left talking quietly in another part of the house. The firetruck had left. The sirens and cell phones had ceased.

But my brain whirled with doubt and uncertainty. I had started the day out as a struggling journalist and, in the space of twenty-four hours, I had added murder suspect to my resume.

Welcome to paradise.

It was almost eleven o'clock by the time I pulled into the Twin Palms RV Resort at Mango Bay. My home. A small, tucked-away RV park, it contained only sixty sites with full hook-ups, a tiny strip of sand that passed for a beach, two shuffleboard courts, and an activities center for the retiree "full-timers" who stayed here for long stretches.

The social scene consisted of various geriatric activities including bingo night and potluck Sunday dinner where the resident seventysomething ventriloquist would entertain us by singing with his stuffed monkey, Tito. Unfortunately, neither one could carry a tune.

After nine o'clock, the "quiet hour" reigned and, since it was off-season and after nine, the place seemed practically comatose. That was fine with me tonight.

Utterly spent, I parked in the designated spot next to my gleaming silver antique Airstream. Just looking at it lightened my mood. Thirty feet long and built in the seventies, its all-metal, all-aluminum construction, all-riveted body, and all-steel undercarriage reigned supreme among the modern trailers and motorhomes on the road today.

I had bought it seven years ago, spent three years

renovating, and lived the life of a gypsy ever since. I could go anywhere in my Airstream with my trusty teacup poodle by my side. I loved the freedom.

Dragging myself out of Rusty, I made for the door of my mobile haven when I heard a rustling sound. I halted. Slowly, I swiveled my head in the direction of the sound, a shadow of alarm passing through me. It was dark at the campsite, but I could make out a large areca palm, its long fronds brushing against the roof of my Airstream. I exhaled in relief.

For safety's sake, though, I scanned the rest of the site. Everything looked normal. My blue and white striped awning flapped in the light evening breeze. My wooden picnic table sat in the same position under the awning. The folding chairs still faced east where I had sat this morning to watch the sun rise as I drank my three cups of heavily-caffeinated, highly-sugared coffee.

The spanking-new, quarter-of-a-million-dollar, class A mega-motorhome was still parked next to me, but no sign of the inhabitants. I hadn't seen them since they'd arrived at the Twin Palms two days ago. The back of the motorhome had JUST MARRIED splashed across the rear window and, true to newlyweds, they seemed to have more than enough cozy pastimes to occupy themselves inside their motorhome.

Most of the other sites around me were empty as they had been this morning. Nothing had changed or been disturbed.

Except me.

I'd come to Coral Island because I wanted to start a new life, find some sense of stability in my existence. Put roots down for a change. But nothing was turning out like I'd planned.

"Hey, Mallie."

I peered through the darkness to see Wanda Sue strolling toward me, her neon spandex shorts with matching top forming a beacon in the night. She was the owner of Twin Palms RV Resort and, from what I'd been able to observe, one of the biggest all-time gossips on the island. "Hi."

"I heard about Jack Hillman. Can you believe it? Someone actually killed him." She clucked her tongue and shook her head, the upswept beehive hairdo remaining firmly in place.

I blinked in amazement, both at her words and the bright yellow color of her outfit. It radiated more wattage than a three-way bulb. "How did you hear about it already?"

"My friend, Joanna, works at the fire department. She heard it from the guys."

"Oh." What could I say? It was a small island.

"Nothing like that ever happens on quiet ole Coral Island. You could've knocked me down with a feather when I heard the news."

"Me too."

"And you were the one to find him?" Her voice turned sympathetic.

"Joanna told you that too?"

She nodded. "Poor you." Her voice turned sympathetic. "That must've been a shock like all getout. Why, I would've been shaking in my shoes and scared half out of my wits."

"It was pretty upsetting." If I turned into a motor mouth when I was excited or nervous, Wanda Sue turned into a cliché convention when she latched onto a juicy tidbit of scandal.

"I gotta tell ya, I'm not surprised, though."

"What do you mean?"

Wanda Sue leaned in closer, her voice lowering into hushed tones. "It was only a matter of time before someone did Hillman in."

"Really?" My interest sparked. "He had a lot of enemies on the island?"

"Enemies? Honey, they were practically hanging from the trees like snipers. If I'd been him, I would've never left my house without one of them bullet-proof vests that SWAT-team guys wear."

"I heard he had a reputation as a womanizer." I dropped the words as if they were a baited hook, just waiting for Wanda Sue to chomp and take off.

"Womanizer?" She laughed with a loud, short laugh. "That man had more women than a dog has fleas. And they weren't all his, if you get my meaning."

"Can you give me any names?"

Wanda Sue tapped her chin. "He has some young blond writer hanging around now—"

"Chrissy?"

"Yep, that's her name. But before her, there was Nora Cresswell—wife of a local fisherman. Her husband, Pete, ran a shrimp boat." She reached into her shirt pocket and pulled out a roll of Lifesavers. "Unfortunately, he hired some guys who did illegal fishing and the Coast Guard arrested the lot of them. When Pete was in jail, Hillman moved in on Nora."

"Nice timing."

"She wasn't the first." Wanda Sue popped a wintergreen mint into her mouth.

"What happened to Nora?"

"She's living on her own—"

A scratching sound interrupted our conversation.

"Ohmygosh, I forgot about Kong," I exclaimed, reaching for the door of my Airstream. As soon as I opened it, my tiny apricot-colored teacup poodle bounded down the stairs and started circling Wanda Sue as he growled low in his throat, at least what could pass for a growl from a three-pound hairy mop of a pooch. "I'm sorry. He gets a little crazed when he's cooped up too long."

I grabbed the leash that I'd left on the picnic table and hooked it on his collar.

"Of course he does, honey. You take him for a walk and put that scoundrel Hillman right out of your mind," Wanda Sue said. She leaned down and attempted to pat him on the head. He growled louder. "What a sweet doggie."

He stomped his miniscule paws on her feet.

"Kong, stop that." I jerked on his leash, knowing his next move would be to nip at her heels. Kong—short for King Kong—didn't like being patronized by humans who wanted to pet him because he was so tiny. When he was a puppy, I'd taken him to a dog psychologist who said Kong suffered from low self-esteem and needed to feel important. That's why he acted aggressive with most people—especially those with a condescending air. So I named him King Kong, hoping to give him a boost. But so far, it wasn't working too well.

"He's really wound up tonight."

"I understand, honey. My cat, Riley, acts the same way when I don't pay enough attention to him. Give him a lot of love and support, and he'll be fit as a fiddle." She tottered off on her high heels.

I looked down at Kong's spunky face and floppy white ears. "Is that what you need? Lots of love and support?"

He wagged his tail.

"Come on, let's head for the beach." I led him toward the Gulf of Mexico, tugging at his leash. For some reason, Kong didn't like the beach. Maybe the expanse of water exacerbated the low self-esteem problem, maybe he didn't like the sound of the waves, or maybe he was just being difficult. At any rate, he resisted all the way to the surf and, once there, sniffed the water as if it were a noxious odor.

"You're going to have to get used to the beach, Kong. This is home." He turned up his brown eyes and button nose in a pleading gesture, then slowly sat down on the sand.

Sighing, I listened to the gentle swell of waves as they rolled ashore. Deep, drawn-out echoes against the soft sand, as if to remind me that a terrible thing had occurred. A man had been murdered tonight and I found his body. I was a suspect.

I knew what my family would say: Mixed-up Mallie had really done it this time. I was on the edge of yet another calamity and this one was a doozy.

Kong wasn't the only one who needed love and support right now. I could use a strong shoulder to lean on. But there was no one in my life.

I was on my own.

Chapter Three

Surprisingly, I enjoyed a heavy, dreamless sleep—probably out of sheer exhaustion. And the next morning I awoke to a bright sun, promising a day of light and warmth. Actually beyond warmth. It would probably hit the upper eighties by midday and my nose would be peeling like the bark on a gumbo limbo tree.

I knocked off my bike path story on my battered laptop computer, took Kong for a brief walk—avoiding the beach—and drove to the *Observer* office. When I walked in the door, Anita was waiting for me, cigarette in hand. A flicker of sympathy in her eyes told me she'd already heard the news. I marveled again that this island had a grapevine unparalleled by none—not even the one Marvin Gaye and Gladys Knight sang about.

"How are ya doing?" she asked.

"Okay. Yesterday was rough, but I'm feeling a little better this morning." I poured a cup of coffee for myself—my fourth already for the day—and added two packets of sugar. Sandy sat at her desk with her eyes closed as she listened to her morning meditation on her iPod. She wasn't wearing a price tag on her slate blue blouse and matching skirt, so I supposed they were keepers. Must be the stretchy jersey fabric.

"I've got to go over to the island police station this morning and give a statement. Do you think I'm dressed okay?" I smoothed down my pea green shirtwaist dress. Being a jeans and T-shirt kind of girl, I'd had to hunt in my closet for one of the few dresses I owned—a gift from my older sister who kept trying in vain to get me into a more conservative style of clothing.

"Yeah, you'll win the fashionista award," she said dryly. "Do you want me to call an attorney?"

My hand tightened around the cup. "Do I need one?"

Anita shrugged. "You were the one that found the body. That means you're a . . ."

"Suspect. I know. But I'm innocent. I didn't even *know* Jack till yesterday. And *you're* the one who sent me there." I flashed a narrow-eyed glare at her.

"True." Ignoring my accusatory eyes, she took a long, meditative drag on her cigarette. "You should be all right since Nick Billie is handling the case. He's a straight-shooter."

"You know him?" Heat crept into my cheeks. Just the mention of his name made my heart beat a little faster.

"Sure do. I've been editing this weekly rag for almost twenty years. There isn't anybody on the island that I don't know, haven't heard about, or written up in the paper—including Nick."

"How long has he lived here?"

"He was assigned as chief detective of island police about five years ago. Before that, he was a tribal police officer."

My interested sparked even higher. "I *thought* he looked Indian."

"Native American is the preferred term today— remember that if it comes up in a news story." She pointed a warning finger at me. I nodded, not wanting to stop the flow of information about Detective Billie. "Nick's a Miccosukee. He grew up on the reservation south of Naples and was involved with a case there a while back that turned ugly. The case was never solved, and he left."

"What was the case?"

"I don't know the particulars. It had something to do with the kidnapping of a young boy."

"How was Detective Billie . . ."

"Forget it—ancient history." She waved her hand and shook her head. "That's not your main concern right now. We've got a murder to cover, and you have a prime opportunity to write the story of your life."

"What about the bike path article?" I held up my finished copy.

She cleared her throat with a scoffing sound. "That's back-page drivel right now. Our lead story is going to be Hillman's murder. And who better to write it than the person who found his body?"

I chewed on my lower lip. "Look, Anita, I might be in a little over my head. I mean . . . I'm a suspect."

"A mere technicality." She waved her hand. "You can do it. You've just got to believe in yourself."

Those words sank in like weights falling to the bottom of the sea. I felt them dropping inside of me with a distinct thud that reverberated through my being. *Believe in myself*. That was what I'd been trying to do most of my life and, so far, I hadn't been exactly successful.

"When you meet with Nick, give your statement, but tell him that you're also going to be covering the story for the paper and you'd appreciate any sharing of information. Then we'll start doing background work on Hillman. We want to give our readers a sense of who he was, and why his death was such an . . . an untimely, tragic event." She enunciated the last part with theatrical flare. "They'll eat it up."

Heartless hag. "There seem to be any number of people who might've had a legitimate reason for wanting him dead." I thought back to the four stricken faces around the table at Hillman's house. All of the writers sitting there probably had grounds for murder. And then there was the wronged husband Wanda Sue had told me about.

"Unexpected then. No one imagines something like that can happen on a quiet little place like Coral Island."

At that point, Sandy removed her headset. She exhaled in a long, musical note as her eyelids fluttered open. Her eyes misted over with contentment and her mouth turned up in a blissful smile. "What did I miss?"

"Hillman's murder," I supplied.

"Old news." She opened her desk drawer and pulled out a small plastic bag that contained exactly two ounces of lowfat cheese and some saltine crackers. "If he'd been aware of the auras around him, he might not have been killed."

"He didn't strike me as the sensitive, New age type." I drained my coffee cup.

"His loss." Sandy shrugged as she nibbled a piece of cheese.

"I want the murder story on my desk by the end of the week." Anita stubbed out her cigarette in a paper cup. "That way, I can edit it and we'll be able to make the deadline. Whadaya say? Are you up to it, kiddo?" She tilted her head to one side and pursed her mouth.

"I'll try." I hated being called kiddo, but it was mild compared to the names she had for other people. None of them exactly nice.

"If you're going be a journalist, you've got to put your feelings on the back burner for the sake of the story. And forget logic. Forget reason. Follow the money," her voice hardened. "Some stories will upset you, wring your stomach inside out, but you've got to turn out copy— that's the important thing. That's the *only* thing."

And that's what I'd need to do to keep my job, I finished for her silently. The implication was clear. Do the story or she'd find someone else who would.

I set my chin in a determined line and summoned what I hoped sounded like a confident tone. "Okay. I'll have something ready for you in a day or two."

"Good. I'm counting on you."

Half an hour later, I pulled into the police station parking lot, already back to my normal unsure self. I'd never given a statement before, and knowing my propensity to become a motor mouth when I was nervous, I was even more uneasy. Just keep it under control, I told myself. Explain what happened and provide only details that are absolutely necessary.

As I walked into the building, my eyes widened in surprise. Instead of the gray walls, functional furniture, and grim faces I expected in a police station, the place had a pleasant air with wood floors and bright yellow walls. A pretty receptionist with a smooth black bob and perky smile sat at the front desk.

"May I help you?" she inquired.

"I'm Mallie Monroe." I hitched my canvas shoulder bag higher on my shoulder. "I have to give a statement."

"Oh, yes, Detective Billie's expecting you." She picked up her phone and pressed a button. After murmuring a few words, she hung up. "He'll be with you in a few minutes. Why don't you take a seat and have a cup of coffee?" She pointed to the large coffeemaker.

I was tempted. Really tempted. But one more cup and I'd be on a total caffeine buzz, and that was the last thing I needed right now. *Think calm, cool, and collected.*

I sat down on a brown leather sofa and started leafing through an old copy of some car magazine that explored the merits of the electric-powered vehicles over the internal combustion machine. Not that I could afford a new car, either electric or gasoline driven, but it was nice to dream a little. And distract myself.

"Ms. Monroe, please come in," Nick Billie said from the door of his office.

He was wearing a pin-striped navy suit this morning and a burgundy tie. It was a more formal look than last night's, but no less attractive. If anything, in his suit he looked more handsome—and more formidable. I was glad I'd chosen the preppy dress—my sister would be proud.

I trailed him into his office and seated myself in a comfortable chair across from his desk. I put my hands in my lap so I wouldn't grip the armrests.

He opened a manila folder and picked up a silver ballpoint pen. I tried not to notice the way his skin pulled taut over the elegant ridge of his cheekbones or the sensual curve of his lips. He really wasn't my type. I liked men who were sort of freewheeling and quirky in their appearance. Surfer dudes. Wonky artists. Guys who lived for sunsets, hammocks, and long afternoons dreaming by the sea. Nick seemed like an unyielding by-the-book kind of guy, but for some reason, I found those qualities strangely attractive in him.

"Ms. Monroe?"

"What? Sorry. I was a little distracted." How about a lot distracted?

He fastened his sharp, penetrating stare on me. "This is a very serious matter. It's a murder investigation, and I need every bit of information that I can get from you to help me solve the case. Do you understand?"

"Yes, of course." Giving myself a mental shake, I cleared my mind of everything besides the murder. Needless to say, not a pleasant thought.

"Now, if you could tell me exactly what happened yesterday from the moment you met Hillman to the time you returned to his house and found him dead." He pushed a small tape player across the desk. "Just speak slowly and clearly, and I'll have our secretary transcribe your statement later. Then you can look it over and see if there are any changes you want to make. Okay?"

"Okay." I cleared my throat a couple of times. It seemed as though my windpipe was closing up and, when I started speaking, my voice sounded unnaturally strained. I'd never had to speak into a tape recorder like this before and I was very conscious of enunciating every syllable.

Eventually, I relaxed into a comfortable rhythm and

relayed everything that had occurred the previous day—leaving out my anger over Hillman's criticism of my bike path story. Detective Billie listened intently, occasionally jotting down a note in the manila folder.

When I finished, he switched off the recorder. "Thank you. Your statement should be very helpful." His tone was brusque, all business.

What did I expect? That he'd be bowled over by the impeccable quality of my memory? That he'd find my red hair suddenly irresistible? That he'd tell me I wasn't really a suspect? Hope springs eternal, even for me.

"One thing—you said last night that Hillman critiqued the writers in the Institute and they appeared . . . disturbed. Does that include everyone?"

I hesitated. "Some of them. I think Chrissy was probably the most upset." Although shy George did have his fists clenched.

"How upset?"

"She started crying after Hillman left the room. The other writers seemed to take it in their stride—especially Burt and Betty." No doubt fortified by the margaritas.

He scribbled down everything I was saying.

"How about you? Were you angry?"

"A little." My windpipe started to close again. I coughed a couple of times and cleared my throat. "But not enough to kill him. I mean, it was only a bike path story."

"True." Detective Billie tapped his pen against his cheek and regarded me with a deep, long look. "You said that Hillman was on the cell phone right before you left. Did you hear him mention the name of the person he was talking to?"

"No."

"And when you left, Chrissy Anders was going out to the hottub to join him?"

"Yes." So far so good. The motor mouth was under control. "That means she might've been the last person to see him alive, right?"

"Possibly."

"So then you'll be questioning her too?"

"Certainly."

"Who else will you be talking to?"

He set the pen down. "Who's doing the interview here, Ms. Monroe?"

"Just curious. And since I'm the main reporter for the *Observer*, I'll be the one to write the story—"

"Hold it right there. Did Anita tell you that I'd share information with you or some such kind of foolishness?"

I smiled.

His straight, dark brows leveled into a severe line. "Look, Ms. Monroe, I don't involve civilians on murder cases and I certainly don't give possible suspects information about the case they're connected with." He flipped the manila file shut. "Anita knows that. She still thinks she's working on the *Detroit Free Press* or something. The reality is this is a small island and she's the editor of a small-town weekly. Murder cases are out of her league—and yours."

My smile faded as irritation flared inside. I might not be the most ambitious person or the most organized, but it rankled when someone told me that I couldn't do something. That made me *really* want to do it. So what if Detective Billie was a handsome hunk? He didn't have the right to order me around. "Maybe the *Observer* isn't some big-time newspaper, but it's where I work and I've got to keep my job. Anita told me to cover the story and that's what I'm going to do—with or without your help."

"Without, I think."

"Then I'll just have to dig for information on my own." I tossed my hair back in a gesture of defiance.

His lips thinned with irritation and he ignored my hair. *Damn.*

"This isn't a game, Ms. Monroe and you're not working at Disney World any longer."

"You checked up on me? My work history?" I asked, incredulous.

"Of course. Standard procedure." He held up the manila folder and, for the first time, I noted that my name was written on the tab. Mallie Monroe. Typed, no less.

I flinched inside at the thought of my life being an open book to anyone who happened to pick up that file—especially Detective Billie. "I thought the police were supposed to cooperate with the media."

"We are, but when the media contact is the person who found the body, it makes things a little tricky— even though your alibi at Capt'n Harry's panned out."

"You already checked that too?"

He nodded. "I'll issue a press release when the time is right." His voice was firm, final. "But this murder investigation is just starting, and I can't let anything or anyone interfere with doing my job."

"But *I've* helped *you* by telling everything I remember that happened on the day Hillman died," I reminded him. "The least you could do is fill me in on what *you* know."

"No deal."

I folded my arms across my chest. "Are you always this rigid?"

"I'd call it professional."

"How about unyielding?"

"Competent?" he offered.

"Stubborn," I came back.

Surprisingly, he laughed—a warm and full-hearted sound that came up from his throat like bubbling, rich oil from deep in the earth. "You're rather tenacious yourself, Mallie."

"About some things—like keeping my job," I said, dropping my hands to his desk, palms down. "If you've got a file on me, then you know I've had a problem settling into something permanent. My last job . . . uh . . . didn't exactly work out. Before I came to Orlando I was a substitute teacher in Atlanta. Before that, a dog trainer in Asheville. Before that—well, I don't remember." Actually, I did remember. I'd been working as a singing waitress at the King's Table Medieval Dinner Club. Unfortunately, I got fired after tripping and spilling a flagon of mead on a customer. I could only hope Detective Billie didn't have that little gem in his file on me.

"It seems like you've been working your way south," he said.

"You could say that. My great-aunt got me this job on the *Observer*, and I really want to keep it. I'm thirty-one years old and all I have to my name is an antique Airstream trailer and a teacup poodle." I met his glance squarely. "I need to show Anita that I can do this job . . . so how about giving me a helping hand? Besides, the paper could actually assist you catch the murderer—involve the entire community. Like those TV programs where they end up catching the criminal because viewers call in with information."

"You can get a real head of steam going when you want to."

"That's me—the Mallie Express." I leaned forward even further. "What about the Sunshine Law? Isn't this information public record?"

"Not in an ongoing investigation."

I shot him a pleading glance.

"All right. I understand that we can help each other here, but I have to be careful not to step outside of police procedure." He picked up his ballpoint pen and clicked it half a dozen times while a little muscle worked in his jaw. "I can share only facts that won't compromise my case."

"Thanks." I exhaled in relief as I pulled out my

official reporter's notepad and riffled around in my bag for a pen. I held it poised, ready for action.

Still, he hesitated.

"Come on, let's start with the actual murder. I know Hillman was knifed. I saw the wound in his chest." I swallowed hard at the memory.

"All I can tell you is that Hillman was killed somewhere between five and seven P.M. The murderer must've been someone he knew because there was no sign of a forced entry. Also, it wasn't a robbery because nothing seems to be missing."

I was writing as fast as my fingers could move. "Murder weapon?"

He shook his head. "Can't say."

"Suspects?"

"A whole island."

"Who is going to be questioned—"

"That's all I can say right now. As the investigation proceeds, I'll give out information on a need-to-know basis." His phone rang and he took the call. After a few short, clipped sentences, he hung up. "Gotta go."

"Is it something pertaining to the murder case?"

He stood up, but said nothing.

"Okay, I get the message." I tossed the notepad and pen in my canvas bag and heaved it over my right shoulder. "I'll be in touch."

As I made for the door, he said, "Wait a minute. I had something else I wanted to ask you."

I halted and turned my head in his direction.

"Is your hair naturally that color?"

"Yeah." I grinned. "I thought you hadn't noticed."

"I didn't."

A tiny glow lit inside me as I left his office. I might not have an ally in Detective Billie, but at least he wasn't an enemy.

Chapter Four

The glow lasted all the way back to the *Observer* office where I found Anita absent—gone to lunch—and Sandy at her desk devouring a low-carb, low-cal meal supplement bar. She was just hanging up from yet another call trying to persuade the Coral Island Shrimp House to buy advertising. From the look on her face, the pitch had been less than successful.

"You had a call," Sandy said between bites.

She handed me the message and I saw a familiar name: Chrissy Anders. I phoned her immediately and she told me the writer's group was convening at the Starfish Lodge, the island's only hotel.

I made it there in record time—not just because I wanted to talk to the writers, but I hadn't eaten anything in my rush to finish the bike path story this morning.

The rumbling in my stomach was a distinct sign that I needed sustenance.

The Starfish Lodge had opened about a month before I arrived on Coral Island. It was located on the south end of the island on an isolated patch of land surrounded by mangroves on one side and Coral Island Sound on the other. A long building with a flat roof, it had only eight rooms, but all of them faced the Sound and were furnished with antiques. The Lodge also had a small restaurant with heart of pine floors and a coral rock fireplace with running waterfalls on either side. The building wasn't new. Anita told me it had been built at the turn of the century as one of those experimental utopian communities where everyone was supposed to live in harmony with nature and each other.

The commune ended when the leader mysteriously disappeared one night with the group's savings, and the building changed hands a dozen times before a developer renovated it last year and turned it into a small hotel. So much for peace, love and brotherhood.

I strolled into the restaurant—Starfish Lounge—and found the writers huddled around a table near the back of the room.

As I approached, I could tell from Chrissy's red-rimmed eyes that she'd been crying. Surprisingly, she threw her arms around me.

"Oh, Mallie, isn't it just awful? We heard the news this morning when we showed up at Jack's house." She pulled back and raised a tearstained handkerchief to her face. "The police met us at the door and told us he was . . . dead."

"Do you know what happened?" Burt motioned for me to sit next to him and Betty who were already working on a couple of Bloody Marys. "Rumor has it you found the body."

"It's true." I sat down and plopped my bulky bag near my feet. Chrissy slid into a chair across the table.

"Was it m . . . m . . . murder?" George asked, raking his long hair back from his face. He displayed no red-rimmed eyes. Just an expression tight with strain.

"Apparently." I noted that Betty shot a furtive glance in Burt's direction, but he gave an imperceptible shake of his head. "I gave my statement this morning to the police."

"Do they have any suspects?" Betty took a deep swig of her Bloody Mary.

"Can't really say," I hedged. "My guess is you'll all be questioned as to your whereabouts when Jack was killed."

"I was watching a video on organic farming." Chrissy tucked her hair behind her ears. "Though not the whole time."

"We drove back here to the Lodge for drinks," Burt offered. "Then to our room." Betty nodded in agreement.

Where you both probably passed out, I added silently.

"I took a long b . . . b . . . bike ride," George said.

"Alone?" I prompted.

"Well . . . yes." He raked his hair back again.

A waitress wearing a splashy tropical print shirt with tight jeans appeared at my elbow. I ordered the blueberry pancakes and a yet another cup of coffee.

After she left, I scanned the writers' group. Their alibis were lame, and they looked like they knew it. Chrissy dabbed at her eyes with a shaky hand, Burt and Betty were preoccupied with their drinks, and George seemed very intent on cleaning a spot off the white linen tablecloth. Any of them could've murdered Hillman.

"After I left yesterday, did you notice anything odd?" I asked.

George shook his head, followed by Burt and Betty. Chrissy, however, lowered the handkerchief and pursed her mouth.

"Now that you mention it . . . about twenty minutes after you left, Jack got out of the hot tub. I stayed in to catch some afternoon rays and work on one of my new poems. I was right in the middle of rhyming 'the joys of compost' with 'those who love you the most,' when I heard him yelling at his neighbor—this old guy who has the house right next door. They were really going at it—and it wasn't the first time I'd heard them arguing."

"Could you make out what they said?" I inquired, trying not to conjecture how compost had anything to do with love. Or anything else in the romantic department.

"Not really."

"Think hard, Chrissy. It could be very important," I pressed her.

"Uh . . ." She drummed her fingers against her cheek. "Oh, yes, I *did* hear something." She straightened in her chair. "The old guy mentioned a land survey that Jack had done a week ago. That's what the argument was about. Yeah . . . I remember now . . . Jack told me his neighbor was disputing the property division between their two lots. Jack had staked out where he wanted to put up a fence and the neighbor said it was partially on his lot. The whole thing kinda mushroomed into this running argument—that's why Jack ordered the survey."

"How angry was the neighbor yesterday?" I asked.

She grimaced. "Absolutely livid. I could hear him yelling for almost half an hour."

"B . . . b . . . but that doesn't mean that he'd want to *kill* Jack," George pointed out. "I mean, he made me so angry sometimes, I couldn't see straight."

"You never know," Betty waved her glass. "This neighbor could've gone berserk."

"That's always possible," I agreed, eyeing George. So he had a temper under all that shy diffidence. Was he a ticking time bomb that had finally gone off last night? My musings were interrupted by the waitress who placed a heaping plate of blueberry pancakes under my nose. I doused them in extra sweet maple syrup and dug in.

"Isn't that stuff full of refined sugar?" With obvious distaste, Chrissy wrinkled her nose at my three large pancakes swimming in syrup.

Burt picked up the plastic syrup bottle. "Nope. Worse. See the label? It's artificially sweetened. That can't be good for you."

I was tempted to point out that Bloody Marys weren't exactly part of the four healthy food groups, not to mention contained a high alcohol content, but refrained. Instead, I concentrated on my pancakes and listened. When I was hungry, fortunately my motor mouth shifted into low gear.

Chrissy clucked her tongue. "I never eat processed foods or artificial anything."

"G . . . g . . . good for you." George's eyes kindled in admiration.

I paused, my fork hovering near my mouth. *Was George infatuated with Chrissy?* He was looking at her as if she were the next best thing to sliced bread. And he'd been furious when Hillman caused her to breakdown in tears yesterday. *Motive for murder? Maybe.*

"Aside from Jack's neighbor, did anyone visit the house while all of you were still there yesterday?" I continued eating the pancakes.

"We left shortly after you did," Burt said. Betty nodded in agreement.

"Me too," George managed to get out without a stammer.

Chrissy sighed. "After my poetry session was interrupted, I left. Jack was still arguing with his neighbor, but no one else showed up."

"How come you're so interested?" Burt's tone turned wary.

Uh-oh. "I'm doing a story on the murder for the *Observer,*" I replied, all of a sudden feeling like an insect pinned to the wall by four pairs of razor sharp eyes. "My editor wants it as the lead story for next week's edition, and I've got to come through for her. My job is on the line."

"Oh," Chrissy responded. She nibbled on an all-natural granola bar. "If you need an interview or want to include a picture of me from my blog for the story, I'd be happy to oblige. Anything for Jack."

"Thanks. I might take you up on your interview offer." Anita would probably burn down the newspaper office before she'd let me promote a blog in the paper. "What are all of you going to do now that the Writers' Institute is . . . defunct?"

"We decided to still meet—right here at Starfish Lounge." Burt waved his hand in a wide arc around the table. "We figured that we'd have to give statements to the police and remain on the island for a while, so we thought we might as well keep critiquing each other."

"I have to keep working on my poetry if I want to make my blog a success by the end of the year," Chrissy said.

"I want to keep going on my b . . . b . . . book on shyness," George added.

"And Betty and I have every intention of finishing

our short story collection." Burt gave a broad smile. "We all felt it would honor Jack's memory to keep writing since he believed in us so strongly."

"That sounds like a plan." I smiled back weakly.

"Hey, how 'bout you joining us, Mallie?" Burt said. "We could review your newspaper stories and help you become a better journalist—not that our critiquing skills are in the same league as Jack."

I opened my mouth to dissent, but then closed it again. Coming to the critique sessions would keep me in contact with them, and give me access to any information they might come up with about Jack's murder. "Why not? Count me in."

"Wonderful." Betty clapped her hands. "We'll meet you here tomorrow morning and get started."

Everyone joined in with a chorus of approving exclamations—except Burt. He simply lifted his glass in a silent toast. I swallowed hard, and not because the pancakes were lumpy, but because I had just committed myself to more endless mornings of literary commentary with four strangers any one of whom could've been Jack's murderer. *Oh, goody.*

A few hours later, after hearing the group discuss Chrissy's "Ode to Jack Hillman: Man of the Earth"— written that very morning—I headed back to the Twin Palms Resort for a swim. I needed to feel the cleansing calm of the Gulf of Mexico.

I pulled up to my Airstream, noticing the honeymooning couple next door in the behemoth RV still hadn't made an appearance. They'd opened their awning and put out two padded lounge chairs, but were nowhere to be seen. I sighed. It must be nice to be so in love. I just hoped they had a good AC unit.

Torn between amusement and envy, I entered my Airstream. Kong greeted me with a few happy, high-pitched barks.

"What do you think, Kong?" I looked down at his large brown eyes. "What are the odds that our honey-mooners will actually make an appearance today?"

Kong lowered his snub nose to the floor and crossed his paws in front. I turned my back to him and pulled on my one piece, racerback swimsuit.

"Maybe ten to one?" I slathered on a new sunblock with a SPF of thirty. "Well . . . fifty to one. They're in a top-of-the-line luxury motorhome, after all."

Kong sniffed audibly.

"Okay, one hundred to one . . ."

I fastened a leash on Kong's collar and led him out of the Airstream. He eyed the beach warily. "At least we have each other," I murmured to my pooch as we strolled toward the surf.

That was something wasn't it?

After my swim, with Kong anxiously watching from shore, I decided to follow up on Chrissy's lead about Hillman's argumentative neighbor. He might not have been angry enough to commit murder, but then again, he might've seen the person who did. I threw on my jeans and a fresh T-shirt and drove over to Hillman's house.

As I approached The Mounds, a lump rose in my throat. Was it only last night that I'd driven up to find the house empty and Hillman dead in his study? I shuddered inwardly. It seemed like weeks ago rather than less than twenty-four hours. Then, my eyes followed the yellow tape that the police had strung around his house. DO NOT CROSS. Like I was about to go in that house. Like I'd *ever* want to go in that house again.

I parked Rusty on the street in front of Hillman's house and hiked up toward the low, flat stuccoed dwelling next door. Before I had the chance to make it halfway up the driveway, an elderly man with a gray beard came charging out of the front porch waving a cane.

"That's far enough," he exclaimed. "This is private property, missy."

"I'm from the *Observer* and I'd like to talk to you." I noted the man's plaid shorts, black silk socks and wing tips. This attire was *de rigueur* for retirees on the island. Sometimes they wore a Hanes white cotton undershirt or a striped golf shirt. But Hillman's neighbor had chosen neither—he was shirtless. What was it about the Mounds that seemed to cause men to wander around half naked?

"I've got nothing to say," he grumbled. "I already talked to the police, and the only thing I could tell them is I'm glad somebody finally did that jerk in."

I assumed the "jerk" he was referring to was Hillman.

"That dadblamed troublemaker was the worst neighbor I've ever had—with his loud music and giggling bimbos coming in and out of here at all hours." He shook his head. "My poor little Mabel couldn't take all that noise—it upset her to no end."

"Your wife?"

"My cat."

"Oh." I moved a little closer and quietly reached into my canvas bag for my handy-dandy official reporter's notepad. "What happened?"

"Mabel's whole system was thrown out of whack. She coughed up hairballs something fierce every time Hillman had a party." He clucked his tongue and pulled on his gray beard.

"That must've been very upsetting." My fingers fished around in the jumble, and I made a vow for the hundredth time to clean out the black hole that passed for my bag.

"I was half crazy. And would that good-for-nothing Hillman even listen? No way. He didn't care if my Mabel's little heart gave out while choking on those hairballs."

"Is she all right now?"

"She's holding her own." He held up a hand to shield his wrinkled forehead from the afternoon sun as he fastened a speculative gaze on me. "You must be a cat person."

"Let's just say I'm an animal person." Actually, I was

allergic to cats—big time. "I'm Mallie Monroe." I held out my hand.

"Everett Jacobs." He kept his hand firmly fixed to his forehead.

"Pleased to meet you." I waved my fingers in lieu of shaking hands. "And my best wishes for Mabel's speedy recovery."

"She'll be fine now that things are quiet again." A note of triumph entered his voice. Was he so obsessed about his cat that he'd actually kill to protect her good health? It hardly seemed possible. But, then again, Everett certainly gave the impression of being a cranky old codger who might not need much of a push to become a vindictive old killer. "I heard that you and Mr. Hillman had some kind of dispute over the boundary line—"

"He was fixing to encroach on my property." The old man's arm came down, hand curled into a fist. "I saw him out here one day with a surveyor and I knew what the two of them was up to."

"But why would he want part of your land?"

"He said it was for some damn privacy fence, but I think he wanted things that weren't his—that's just how he was. But I wasn't about to give him one foot of my property. I already lost part of my acreage to that Henderson Research Center."

My ears perked up. "Research Center?"

"Yep." He pointed to the back of his property where the shell mounds were the highest. "Some archaeologists from the University of Florida got a grant to go digging up there, and I had to let 'em—something about the area being declared a historic site. Next thing I know people are poking around at all hours, turning up things they shouldn't be messin' with."

"That's an archaeological dig?" I followed his glance toward the highest mound and noticed a roped off area on the top. "I had no idea."

"Well, now you know, missy." He emitted a loud cackle and wagged his head. "The only good thing is they also dug up Hillman's part of the mound, too. He didn't like it anymore than I did."

"So you had something in common."

"Yeah, we hated trespassers." His fierce old eyes fastened on me again. *Yikes!*

"Would you mind if I took a look at the dig?"

"Why?"

I smiled, stalling for time until I could think of a good reason. "I've never seen one before." Oh, wow, was *that* a compelling reason. I mentally kicked myself for the lame excuse, but I never was good at lying. Maybe that's why I wasn't as successful as my sister. I could never fib enough to get the kind of job where you had to stretch the truth so thin just to make it through the day that reality became a distant dream. It had been hard enough for me to tell people "Welcome to the Magic Kingdom—Where You'll Have the Time of Your Life," when I knew the reality was that they'd be dragging screaming kids around with them for ten hours and then stagger back to their hotels as food-splattered, foot-aching zombies.

I waited to see if Everett would order me off his land faster than you could say "burial mound."

"All right, but don't whine if the prickly pears scratch your arms to smithereens."

"I'll be careful." But I'd also be sniffing around. Maybe something about the dig held a clue to Hillman's murder.

Everett turned on the heels of his scuffed wingtips and motioned for me to follow with his gnarled old cane. We started up a narrow shell path flanked on either side by gumbo limbo trees and huge bougainvillea bushes. An occasional prickly pear cactus stretched its long, thin barbs toward my arms, but I successfully dodged most of them. Higher and higher, we climbed. Perspiration beaded on my forehead and my breath came in ragged gasps but, surprisingly, my intrepid guide scrambled up the path with the alacrity of a mountain goat—even in his unsuitable footgear. When we reached the top, I bent over and took in a couple deep breaths.

"Looks like you need to work up a sweat a little more often, missy," Everett said. He wasn't even breathing heavily. *Old coot.*

"Seems so." Breathe in, breathe out. Whew. The oxygen struggled to get into my lungs, but they weren't used to that much exertion and almost screamed in outrage.

Okay, I know I should exercise more, but marching on a treadmill wasn't my idea of fun, and I wasn't outdoorsy.

Gradually, my breathing settled down and I could take stock of my surroundings.

We were standing about thirty feet above the shoreline on a giant mound of crushed shells and, as I scanned below, I realized I could see almost from one end of the island to the other. "This is incredible. I can make out Mango Bay."

"Nothing to see there but a bunch of tourists and fishermen." He pulled a red bandana out of the back pocket of his shorts and blew his nose in a loud, honking sound. *Charming.* "I try not to drop into Mango Bay but once a week."

"Probably just as well," I mumbled. Strolling around the top of the mound, I halted in front of the neatly roped off area. The dig comprised about a twenty-foot square, with a depth of maybe ten feet. It didn't look like much more than a big hole with bits of black pottery and broken shells at the bottom. I sighed in disappointment. There was nothing up here to provide clues to Hillman's murder. People generally don't kill for pottery chips. "It's not . . . much, is it?"

"Actually, it's quite an important site," a quiet voice said from behind me.

I turned and spied a man approaching with stiff dignity. He wore neatly pleated dress pants, a polo shirt and loafers. On his head he sported a wide-brimmed straw hat. "This mound used to be almost sixty feet high with a canal at the base that led to the Sound."

"Wow."

"Hello, Everett," the man said. "Is everything going well?" Probably in his mid-thirties and small-boned; of medium height, he had a beaklike nose and wore thick, square glasses that seemed too large for his thin face.

Everett mumbled something that could have been "hello" or "hell no." I supposed the latter.

"Mr. Jacobs brought me up here to see the dig."

"If you want to know more about the site, you can take a tour. The Henderson Research Center gives a two hour presentation on the dig and their findings."

"Do you work for them?"

He nodded. "I chair the board that oversees the dig and I also run the Coral Island Historical Museum." He stretched out a hand. "Bradley Johnson."

"Mallie Monroe. I work for the—"

"*Observer*," he finished for me. "I've seen your by-line on the bike path stories."

I groaned.

"Hey, that's important news on Coral Island. We all want that bike path to happen." He grinned and I noticed a slightly crooked front tooth. "You doing a story on the dig?"

"No—I just wanted to see it."

"People shouldn't be digging on the mounds, disturbing history." Everett kicked a couple shells with the toe of his shoe.

"But this is an important site—archaeologically speaking, of course," Bradley protested.

"Who built the mounds?" I asked, wondering if Everett should actually be kicking artifacts around as if they were crumbled pieces of garbage.

"The ancient Caloosa Indians," Bradley informed me. "They lived here about five thousand years ago and built these for their villages and temples. Pretty ingenious really. They hauled tons of sand and shell to build their mounds and the sides were held in place with rows of white conch shells. At the base of the mounds there was an intricate system of canals so they could canoe between villages."

"And if they were high and dry up here they were protected from the storms and high water," I reasoned. "So why are the mounds only about half as tall?"

"Early homesteaders on the island removed the top layers of sand and shell shell to build roads on the island." His voice took on an indignant tinge. "Imagine that. Disturbing an ancient archaeological site to build a stupid road."

"People had to get around the island. In those days it was tough going," Everett chimed in. He was now picking up shells and tossing them toward the shoreline below.

"It must've been so peaceful and unspoiled when the Caloosa lived here." I could almost envision these ancient Indians living a quiet life, fishing and living off the land.

"It wasn't exactly like that." Bradley shattered my pastoral fantasy. "The Caloosa were warriors—six feet tall and covered with tattoos. They raided neighboring villages constantly and took their captives as slaves."

"Did they trade in gold?"

"Nope . . . shells were their currency."

No treasure. No gold. And no motive up here to kill Hillman. "At least they didn't practice human sacrifice or anything," I joked.

Bradley's face grew somber. "I'm afraid to say they did."

I grimaced. *There goes paradise.*

"Seems like a practical way to get rid of people you don't like," Everett said.

Bradley laughed. "And I suppose you'd start with the archeaologists up here."

"Maybe. Like I said, they're meddling in things that's better left alone."

"The research foundation is doing everything it can to maintain the integrity of the mounds." Bradley gestured toward the neatly roped-off area.

"It's *my* land and I should have the final say so about what's done on it," Everett bristled.

Bradley blinked several times in rapid succession and pushed the glasses higher on his nose. "I thought you and Hillman jointly owned this mound."

"We do. This blasted dig sits smack dab in the middle of our property line," Everett spat out. "Not that Hillman recognized it. He was trying to get some surveyor to cheat me out of my land, but nothing was settled." His mouth took on an unpleasant twist. "Leastwise, he won't be able to argue about it with me anymore."

"Did you two finally settle your differences?" Bradley asked.

"Oh, yeah. Everything's settled all right."

"Really? I'm so glad you—"

"They haven't agreed on anything," I cut in. "Mr. Jacobs is referring to the fact Jack Hillman died last night."

"Good god." His eyes widened behind the glasses. "What happened? I mean, I didn't even know he was ill."

"He wasn't," I said grimly. "Someone murdered him."

Bradley's mouth gaped open. "Murder? I don't believe it. Who would want to kill him?"

"Pick a number and stand in line," Everett quipped.

"The police are investigating and questioning everyone who knew him." I chose to ignore Everett's rude interruption, but made a mental note of it. Everything he's said so far made him my number one suspect. He hated Hillman and seemed just ornery enough to kill him. "I'm actually doing a story about his death for the *Observer.* Do you have any comments?" I brought out my notepad and poised my pen above it.

"Uh . . . no. Well, yes, I suppose I'm shocked and dismayed that anything like that could happen on Coral Island. And, of course, the loss of Jack Hillman will be felt far and wide in the writing community—both here and elsewhere across the country."

"She asked for a comment, not a speech," Everett said.

"That's what I'm doing, damn it," Bradley replied, his eyes kindling in sudden anger. "Jack was a friend of mine and I, for one, will miss him sorely. He donated generously to the museum and frequently did public appearances for fund-raisers." Bradley removed his hat and waved it back and forth in front of his face. "Have a little respect, will you?"

"Respect is for them that earns it." Everett's eyes hardened. "As far as I'm concerned Hillman could've been one of those ancient sacrifices you were jabbering about. Maybe those Caloosas didn't have such a bad idea. I don't think they sacrificed victims to their gods— they were probably getting rid of people who'd become public nuisances."

"Everett, you're a surly old curmudgeon," Bradley exclaimed.

"So tell me something I don't know. At least I'm not pretending to mourn someone who I didn't give a rat's patootie about."

I took a glance at the old man's face. His mouth, outlined by his beard, was set in a mutinous line. His eyes hard and cruel. An oddly primitive warning sounded off in my brain, and I was grateful that Bradley had showed up. At that moment, Everett looked just mean enough to commit murder.

"Do you know if the police have any leads?" Bradley replaced the hat on his head.

"I'm not sure," I evaded an answer, stepping away from Everett. "Detective Nick Billie is handling the case."

Silence descended on our little group, the shadow of murder hovering over us. Everett had resumed kicking shells and Bradley seemed lost in his own thoughts. I was struggling hard not to remember the sights and smells of death that I'd seen last night. No matter what I did to keep a lid on the memories, they kept surfacing, rising to the top like debris from the darkest regions of the ocean floor.

Maybe it was this place. It was already filled with ghosts. All the lost souls of the long-dead Caloosa who'd lived and died here. The shells and the mounds were a mute testimony from another time . . . and a civilization destined not to survive.

"What happened to the Caloosa?" I finally asked, attempting to divert my thoughts.

Bradley looked out at the water of Coral Island Sound. "When the Spaniards came, they brought their diseases with them. Smallpox, yellow fever, measles—you name it—the Caloosa had no immunity. They were wiped out in probably less than a century. Some might've made it to the Everglades where they intermarried with the Miccosukee, but no one knows for sure."

"Except that they're gone." My words echoed around the stillness.

Everett emitted a scoffing sound. "When the dead are dead, there's nothing you can do to bring them back.

No good comes from poking around, except stirring up all kinds of bad feelings that could end up causing more harm."

Everett shot a glance in my direction. *Was that a warning? Was I bringing harm on myself by asking too many questions?* I didn't dare inquire. I was afraid what I would hear.

Chapter Five

By midmorning the next day I wasn't thinking about the Caloosa Indians or crusty old Everett Jacobs. I'd been trying to pound out the Hillman story at the *Observer* office with Anita breathing down my neck.

"Haven't I told you a hundred times you've got to include a strong hook in the first paragraph?" Anita grumbled, her cigarette bobbing up and down with each word.

"I thought I did." I pointed at the first paragraph on my computer screen.

"Think again." Anita leaned in closer and I couldn't help it—I inhaled. Something else besides the usual smoky haze emanated from her. I took a surreptitious whiff. Then another. What was that smell? I couldn't quite place it. Then I realized—gasoline. She must've hit the self-serve pump at the Circle K—the only place to get gas on the island. Smoke and gasoline made a heady combination first thing in the morning, to say the least.

"Look at that first sentence," she cut in. "You're using passive voice and too many adjectives. 'Jack Hillman, famous writer of gritty true crime thrillers, was found dead in his Coral Island home in the late evening of June fifth.' Blah. Blah. Blah."

"But I have who, what, when, and where," I protested. "You said those were the important things to include in the first paragraph."

"Yes, but not with passive voice." She thumped the top of the monitor for emphasis. The old computer screen tilted precariously for a few seconds and I raised a hand to steady it.

"All right, I'll tweak it some more. What about the rest of the story?"

"It doesn't exactly stink," she grudgingly admitted.

"Thanks." Hatchet-face, I added silently.

"Look, kiddo, I thought you wanted to be a journalist. If you do, you need to work on your writing. That never ends. It's always progress, not perfection."

I sighed and looked over at Sandy. She offered a sympathetic smile as she downed her third lowfat yogurt of the morning.

"We want the truth about Hillman in this article, but play down the content about his early years as a security guard. No one cares about his experiences keeping the Coca-Cola factory safe for democracy." She hit the scroll button. "The stuff on his literary fame and the Writers' Institute is okay. Then wrap up with Bradley Johnson's comments."

"He was about the only person I talked to who had anything good to say about Hillman."

She shrugged. "Sometimes when you become famous, people get envious. It happens."

"Do you think that's why he was murdered?"

"Nope. Murder takes something stronger—hatred, jealousy, greed—emotions that make your blood boil."

"His neighbor sure seems to hate him," I said.

"Everett?" She waved a hand dismissively. "He's just cranky. Been that way for as long as I've know him. He's threatened to sue practically everyone on the island—including our paper."

"No way."

"Yep. Said we misquoted him on an interview about the excavation of the shell mounds."

"Did you?"

Her thin mouth puckered in annoyance. "If there's one thing I know it's how to quote a source. He was just making trouble."

"I think he's way beyond the 'making trouble' category when it comes to Hillman. Everett hates him."

"We'll see. If he did murder Hillman, we'll be the first to print it. Remember, follow the money," Anita cackled, as she gave me a swift pat on the shoulder. "Back to work, kiddo. I'm going to call the coroner to see if he has any new information." She disappeared into her office.

I made the changes my hard-nosed editor wanted, then decided to check the Internet for any other Hillman interviews. After researching for another hour, I'd found only one other interview he'd given to the *Miami Herald* during the South Florida Library Festival two years ago. I scanned it and stopped in amazement about halfway through.

"Did you ever meet Jack?" I asked Sandy who had finished her yogurt and was now carefully checking to make sure the price tag was tucked into the short sleeve of her soft lavender cotton dress. I eyed the latest addition to her endless parade of temporary clothes with envy. The tag subterfuge provided some distinct advantages. My own meager salary hadn't allowed me to purchase more than my usual uniform of T-shirt and jeans, both of which I wore today.

Maybe I was hallucinating from staring at the computer screen all morning, but she looked a bit thinner.

"I met him several times." She tossed the empty yogurt container in the trash can.

"This article says he volunteered for Big Brothers/Big Sisters and donated a sizable amount of money to help open the Island Museum."

"Oh?"

"Yeah, it's all right here." I pointed at the screen. "He was a Big Brother to an island boy named Todd Griffith for six years . . . the kid's grandmother later took him and his mom in, and he's finishing high school in Miami now. And Hillman also contributed ten thousand dollars to the Island Museum. Wow. He actually did something nice."

"I guess." Sandy shrugged. "It's hard to be impressed with someone who refuses to speak to you."

"You mean he came by the office and ignored you?"

"He sure did—once he got a look at me."

"What are you saying?"

"I'm saying he was prejudiced against overweight women." Her lower lip trembled, but she tightened it in a firm line. "I know the type. They're all sugar sweet over the phone, but when they drop by and see I'm a large gal, they simply pretend I'm not here. Like I'm some kind of piece of furniture or something."

"I . . . I'm sorry," I said. Chalk up another black mark against Jack. So far he had two white marks and a slew of black ones. "Sandy, you know I don't feel that way about you."

"I know." She rearranged the blue ceramic bracelets on her wrist. "In spite of Hillman's 'good works,' I wasn't exactly heartbroken to hear that he'd been killed."

"Welcome to the island club," I muttered.

"Not that I'd do him in, of course. I've dealt with my anger through focused imagery—a technique I read about in one of my self-help books. But I'm telling you, it was incredibly tough to work my way through all the negative emotion that man aroused—I had to use candles, incense, tapes and my special quartz crystal. The works." She spread her arms expansively.

"I'm glad that you were able to . . . uh . . . let it go."

"Me too. Speaking of which. . . ." She reached for her iPod. "I've got to do my morning affirmations."

"Serenity now!" I gave her a peace sign.

She donned the earphones and closed her eyes. In a few minutes, her face took on a peaceful, calm expression. I eyed her with renewed respect—not simply for her ability to sink into a relaxed state amidst a cramped, noisy office, but because she was able to overcome her dislike for a man that half the island probably would've liked to feed to the sharks.

I reread the section in the *Herald* article about Hillman's "Little Brother" and jotted down his grandmother's name. I called Miami information and got a phone number so I could call her later for an interview. Then I made a mental note to visit Bradley and discuss the museum donations.

Intrigued, I realized the "truth" about Jack was taking on interesting and unexpected dimensions.

The door to the office suddenly flung open and I jumped in my chair.

"What did I tell you about interfering with my investigation?" Detective Billie demanded as he slammed the door shut, his dark face set in a mask of cold fury.

"Huh?"

"I just spent an hour on the phone with Everett Jacobs. He said you were nosing around Hillman's house and badgering him with questions." Detective Billie strode toward my desk.

"That's not true." I stood up to meet him when he got there. It didn't help much, though. He was still almost a head taller than me and . . . intimidating to say the least when his eyes blazed down from that impressive height.

"Did you or did you not snoop around Hillman's house?"

"Not. I know better than to cross the yellow tape."

"What about badgering Everett?"

I glanced over at Sandy for support, but she had her back to us with her iPod still running. "I asked him some questions—that's all. I certainly didn't 'badger' him or anything like that. *He* was the one who volunteered information—told me all about Mabel and how Jack had driven her to distraction. Granted, he was sort of grouchy at first, but he gradually warmed up—especially when I showed some sympathy for the Mabel situation. Although if you ask me, he's your number one suspect. He *hated* Hillman—"

"Could you please stick to the subject?"

"I'm trying to." Could I help it my motor mouth was stuck in high gear every time Detective Billie appeared? "Anyway, Everett even took me for a tour of the shell mounds. Would he have done that if I was making a nuisance of myself?"

"Possibly."

"Well, I guess you'll just have to decide who's telling

the truth. The island curmudgeon or me." I folded my arms across my chest and matched him glare for glare.

The muscle in his jaw began working overtime as he digested my words. I decided to press my advantage.

"From what Anita tells me, Everett is a cantankerous old man who likes to cause trouble. I just happen to be the last person who ticked him off. And maybe I did because he's got something to hide. Did you ever think of that?"

"Don't tell me how to do my job. Everett will be questioned as a possible suspect when I say so."

"Are you kidding? He should be at the top of your list."

"That's for me to decide."

I took in a deep breath and tried to adopt a more conciliatory tone. "It seems to me that anyone as mean-tempered as Everett could've easily been pushed over the edge to commit murder."

He weighed me with a critical squint and, gradually, some of the anger faded from his face. "I can't deny that Everett lodges a lot of complaints about fellow islanders."

"See what I mean?"

"But you shouldn't be bothering him in the first place."

"I was only asking him questions about Hillman for my news story."

"You are technically still a suspect even though your

alibi checked out, Ms. Monroe, and that means you need to tread very carefully. If I think or get word that you're trying to manipulate information to your advantage, I'll throw you in jail."

I swallowed hard. Jail. Yikes. That's just what my family needs to hear. Mixed-up Mallie has become a no-account, down-and-out jailbird.

"I won't step over the line," I promised.

"See that you don't."

"And why not? Sometimes lines need to be crossed." Anita stood in the doorway of her office.

Oh, no. And just when I'd calmed down Detective Billie. *Please, Anita, stay out of it.* I silently offered up a prayer to the saint of browbeaten journalists—the one that must've protected Woodward and Bernstein during the Watergate scandal.

"Anita, I'm not going down this road with you," Detective Billie transferred his glance to my boss. Strangely, I'd swear admiration was lit in the depths of his dark eyes. "You know what you can and can't do legally when it comes to a murder investigation."

"Yes, I do. We *can* question people who might have comments about Hillman that we can use in our stories."

"I won't tolerate interference in my job."

"And I won't tolerate your trying to censor freedom of the press."

Watching Anita's leathery face set in stubborn lines, I gave up on the prayers.

The two of them looked like prizefighters squaring off at their side of the ring. Not that they'd come to blows, but the verbal punches packed quite a weight.

"Questioning people for a story is different from trying to get information about the murder out of them." Detective Billie landed a right jab to the side with that one.

Anita remained standing. "Interviewing people isn't against the law. And in the course of questioning them, we can't anticipate that everything they say won't touch on the murder," she countered with her own effective punch.

"Revealing information that could tip off the murderer could blow my whole investigation." He landed a double blow with that one.

"Withholding information from the public could enable the murderer to strike again." Anita went on the offense. "I'm sure that's the last thing you'd want to happen."

"Are you questioning my ability to protect the people of Coral Island?" He did a neat sidestep, but her last punch had obviously winded him a bit.

"Nope. But people need to know the truth." Anita knew she had him on the run now and moved in for the kill. "Then they can protect themselves."

"This kind of murder wasn't a burglary or theft. There's no serial killer lurking in the palm fronds—and to suggest there is could incite people on the island to panic unnecessarily." Detective Billie managed to land a verbal hit dead on target with that one.

Anita turned silent. Detective Billie radiated triumph. I stood in awe. Sandy, of course, had missed the entire match and, unfortunately, I hadn't had the time or forethought to videotape the whole thing for slow-motion replay later.

"We'll conduct ourselves with responsible journalism. I can promise you that." Anita's thin-lipped mouth curved upward on one side, causing the mass of tiny wrinkles around her lips to deepen. She knew she had him. No matter what he threw at her, she'd still be standing.

"I'm going to hold you to that, Anita." Detective Billie's voice held a stern warning.

"You've got it, buddy." She pulled out her pack of Camels and lit up.

"What about Ms. Monroe?"

"What about her?"

"Yeah, what about me?" I finally found my voice.

"You need to make sure that she understands the boundaries of what she can and can't do on an interview." He flicked a hand in my direction.

"I told you, Everett volunteered the information he gave me," I insisted, heartened by Anita's recent victory. "I repeat, I didn't badger him."

Detective Billie swung his attention back to me. His straight, black eyebrows were no longer leveled in an angry line. "Okay, Ms. Monroe. I believe you, but I'm also warning you to keep your interviews on the up and up—no information about the murder leaked to the public without police consent."

"Sure." I nodded for emphasis.

"All right, then." He adjusted his tie and yanked on the sleeves of his jacket. The motions were controlled, but I could sense the frustration behind his movements. He was a rock—with his hard-planed face and obsidian-colored eyes, but Anita was a scrappy, scrawny tree—the kind that bent in the wind, but then righted itself and slapped you in the face. She'd always win because she knew how to deflect the force that came at her. Detective Billie had a bull-like stubbornness that caused him to charge in, head down, face forward. He had integrity, but she had cunning. And cunning would always win out.

"Well, now, that's cleared up, do you have a statement for the press?" Anita inquired as she took a long drag on her cigarette.

A long paused ensued. Then, surprisingly, a low rumble of laughter erupted from Detective Billie. "Nothing at this time."

"I hear you." She winked at him. "See you later, Nick."

"Not if I see you first," he responded, humor still lingering in his face. "By the way, it's illegal to smoke in a public building."

"Uh-huh." She waved him off with her cigarette and returned to her office.

Nick shook his head, then held out a folder in my direction. "I almost forgot. This is a transcript of the statement that you gave to me two days ago. Look it over and see if there is anything you want to change."

"Right now?" I took it from him, carefully avoiding touching his fingers. "I've got a story that I'm on a deadline to finish."

He shrugged. "You can look it over and drop it by the station later."

"Thanks." I knew I wouldn't be able to concentrate on the statement if he loomed over me. I was too aware of him, too distracted by the woodsy scent of his aftershave, too unsettled by his dark eyes.

"Don't let Anita persuade you into doing things that you know are wrong. A newspaper story is one thing but, when it comes to solving a crime, that's police business—period."

"I've got it already. All right?"

"All right." He paused, as though he was going to say something else, but then changed his mind. "Are you doing . . . okay?"

I clutched the folder to my chest. "I guess so—for someone who found a dead body."

"Believe it or not, I understand. Murder is never an easy thing to accept." A shadow passed over his features, completely erasing all traces of humor.

"But you're a cop—you deal with this kind of thing all the time."

"Not really." He shook his head. "Killing people

doesn't happen on my watch—and I don't intend to let it happen again." His voice hardened as his glance caught and held mine captive.

Something turned over inside of me. I wasn't quite sure what it was. It could've been a spark of attraction. Or maybe a flicker of sensual excitement. Or maybe even indigestion. Who knows? But the tremor of emotion behind his words touched me in a way I couldn't pinpoint.

We stood there for a few moments, not moving, our eyes locked together.

"Hey, Nick, how are ya doing?" Sandy finally broke the spell as she spun around in her chair and removed her iPod.

"Fine—I was just leaving," he answered. "Make sure you drop off that transcript, Ms. Monroe." The reserved, by-the-book cop persona was back in place. He strode toward the door and was gone before I could say, "Have a nice day." *Thanks a lot, Sandy.*

"Did I miss anything?" Sandy asked.

I rolled my eyes. "Not really."

"Good." Humming, she put her iPod in the top drawer of her desk. "I was *so* into a deep TM state that time. My new meditation tape is really wonderful—the guy who did it studied at some ashram in India."

"Wow." I didn't know the least bit about ashrams, but I figured it must have something to do with personal growth, weight loss, and/or both.

Sandy's features assumed their usual serene composure. "I'm going to use the computer for awhile, all right?"

"Sure. I have to see someone. Just save what I was working on to the hard drive." I'd wrap it up later. Right now, I needed to talk to the person who I trusted more than anyone on the planet: my great aunt Lily.

Minutes later, I was driving toward the southeast part of the island called Franklin's Grove. My great aunt and several other families had moved there during the 1920s when it was a bustling little settlement, complete with a warehouse on the waterfront, a post office and school. Originally, Aunt Lily and her husband, with four other homesteader families, owned eighty acres. They produced some of the best citrus in all of Southern Florida.

Unfortunately, when the depression hit in the thirties, Franklin's Grove declined.

Most of the families moved away and their groves fell into disrepair, but Aunt Lily stayed. She survived three hurricanes, a world war, and the loss of her husband. But she never gave up her land. About ten years ago, she replaced the citrus with mango and lychee nut trees, tapping the new market for exotic fruit. It wasn't exactly a thriving venture, but she made a living. She got by.

I steered Rusty down the shell and limestone road that led to her house. It stood smack dab in the middle of her grove—a whitewashed, one-storied dwelling with a porch across the front and a tin roof. As soon as I saw the familiar structure nestled among the pine trees, a warm feeling flooded through me, and I remembered why I'd come to the island a month ago with my Airstream and my teacup poodle. This was the only place I'd ever felt a sense of peace as a kid.

The memories of brief summer vacations spent picking fruit rose up in my mind. I could still smell the sweet scent of June bloom oranges as I twisted them off of the branches and tossed them into large wooden baskets. Feel the sensation of heavy, tropical rain when it would plaster my shirt against my chest. Remember what it was like to run barefoot all day and stay up half the night. Earthy. Elemental. Soul-stirring. I was never constrained by rules and manners and the "right" way of doing things like at home.

Needless to say, my parents didn't let me come here all that often and, when I did, they'd spend months "working the Florida taint" out of me.

But now I was here—permanently living in paradise. Sort of. I did have the slight problem of working for a chain-smoking, hatchet-faced editor and being a suspect in a murder investigation. But this is a fallen world afterall. Who's expecting perfection?

I parked Rusty and, before I could shut off the engine, Aunt Lily appeared on the porch.

"Mallie, I've been trying to call you for two days," she exclaimed. A pair of Yorkshire terriers positioned themselves on either side of her and barked their own greeting. We also had something else in common: our love of canine companions.

I climbed out of my truck and took the steps two at a time. "I'm sorry, but I don't have an answering machine yet. I only got a phone hook up two weeks ago." I hugged her, savoring the warm feel of her strong, supple arms. All of a sudden, though, they felt a little thinner to me and I pulled back to get a good look at her. Thick, gray hair worn in a braid and fierce blue eyes. Faded freckles, now merged into the lines around her eyes. A wide, smiling mouth. It was all comfortingly familiar.

But her face did seem a little drawn compared to a couple of weeks ago when I last saw her, the lines a little deeper. A twinge of guilt nagged at me. I hoped I wasn't the cause of those deep worry lines on her forehead.

"So what do you expect?" she asked, as though divining my thoughts. "I'm seventy-eight years old and worried sick about my favorite great niece."

"You don't look a day over sixty."

"Pfffft." She waved a hand. "Flattery will get you everywhere." The dogs kept up their yapping. "Biscuits, Gravy, shut up."

They instantly quieted down.

"I guess I don't need to ask whether or not you heard about Jack Hillman's murder," I said.

"Dreadful man." Her mouth tightened into a thin line. "I remember the last time he gave a talk at my quilter's group—right before the Mango Festival. He went on and on about how the island was becoming too commercial, that developers were ruining the Mounds, that the 'real' Florida was passing away. Hah. Like that's such a bad thing. I'll give him 'real Florida.' I remember when it took a whole day to walk to Mango Bay and we had to wear bee veils the entire way because of the mosquitoes. Those vile creatures were so big you could put a saddle on 'em and ride 'em. Bad roads, hurricanes, oppressive heat. You can have the 'good old days.' " She threw up her hands in disgust.

Did I mention that my aunt also possessed the "motor mouth gene"? In fact, I probably inherited it from her.

"Actually I've been doing some digging and I found out that he wasn't a complete jerk after all. Did you know that he sponsored a kid with Big Brothers/Big Sisters? An island boy who's in Miami now."

"I'd heard about him—Todd something or other." She didn't look impressed. "I guess everyone has a soft side."

"Anybody you know might've had a motive to kill Hillman?"

She cast an ironic glance in my direction. "The real question is who *didn't* have a motive for killing him. Maybe you ought to start from there and eliminate all the people who couldn't possibly have committed murder."

I sighed. "That would be a pretty short list—just you and me."

"Speak for yourself."

"You, too?"

"After ticking off my quilter friends? You'd better believe it, Carrot." A beeping sound went off inside her house. "Oh, just a minute, my cornbread is done. Did you have lunch yet?"

"Nope." I smiled at Aunt Lily's nickname. She christened me "Carrot" when I was a kid—for obvious reasons—and she was the only one I'd let call me that.

"Well, settle yourself down and I'll rustle us up something. I know how you like your food." She winked at me and went into the house. Biscuits and Gravy stayed on the porch, occupied with the complex task of unraveling a ball of white cotton yarn Aunt Lily had left out as a playtoy.

I slid into one of the high-backed wooden rockers, listening to quiet chirping of two scrub jays that perched on my aunt's birdfeeder. They took their fill and then flew off.

A short while later, Aunt Lily reappeared with a tray holding two enormous fruit salads and a generous helping of warm cornbread. She set it on a wicker table between the two rockers and handed me a glass of iced tea—Southern sweet, of course.

"Nothing like a sweet tea on a hot day," she commented as she took a long, deep drink.

"Can't argue with you there." I joined her and took a swig of my iced tea. Then I broke off a chunk of the cornbread and chewed it slowly. "De-lish."

She smiled, flipping her long braid over her shoulder. "Nice to know I haven't lost my touch."

"Never." I leaned my head back. "How *did* you find out about the murder?"

"Wanda Sue told Emily Watson—she works at Whiteside's on the day shift." Aunt Lily arched her brows in delicate emphasis. "From there the story worked its way toward the Island Center where I heard it from the Jordan sisters—you know the two blonds with identical peace sign tattoos on their ankles? Anyway, I overheard them talking at the Island Hardware Store."

I hadn't met the Jordan sisters yet, but I'd be looking for those tattooed ankles.

"All they had were the barest of details. So fill me in."

I took another swallow of my iced tea for fortification. "Let's just say I'm working on a news story for the *Observer* about Hillman's murder, and I'm between a rock and a hard place when it comes to Anita and Detective Billie."

"And what hard place would that be?" She smiled suggestively.

"Aunt Lily—behave."

"Don't tell me you haven't noticed that our friendly island chief deputy is one good-looking man—tall, dark, and handsome, to use a cliché."

"I've noticed." I popped a juicy piece of mango into my mouth. "Not my kind of guy—too uptight. As attractive as Detective Billie is, he's all business when it comes to dishing out information about Hillman's murder. And Anita is just hard headed about the newspaper doing its own investigation." I sighed and shook my head. "I've got to find a way to write my stories without pushing him to the point that he throws me in jail."

Aunt Lily was quiet for a few moments as she stared off toward two large weeping willow trees that arched over the driveway. Their branches actually touched as if they were reaching out to each other. "I've usually found when I'm being pulled in two directions the best thing to do is keep up a good front and just go my own way."

"What do you mean?"

"I mean, find your own path. What do *you* want to do?"

I paused, trying to find the words to voice what I'd been too afraid even to think. "I want to know what happened. It's stupid. I've been at the paper only a month, and I'm totally inexperienced when it comes to this kind of investigative journalism. But it . . . intrigues me."

"Okay then." She tapped her chin meditatively. "Work on the articles Anita assigns, say nothing to Nick Billie, and glean as much information as you can to piece together the truth of what happened that night."

"The whole truth? Is that possible?"

"Maybe—I might be able to help."

"Oh, thank you, Aunt Lily."

"But we'll need a little assistance." She drained the last of her iced tea and dabbed at her mouth with the linen napkin. "It's time to bring in Sam."

"Who's Sam?"

"My handyman." She pronounced the last word as though it was a royal title—perhaps not a monarch, but at least a duke or earl. The Duke of Mango Bay? I swallowed a nervous laugh.

"We might need more than a guy who can fix clogged drains," I said.

"Sam's our man. He's in and out of everybody's house on the island, and he hears more in one day than you'll be able to gather in a week of snooping." She gave me a quick, reassuring smile. "Don't fret, Carrot. I'll go give him a call." She exited the porch.

I picked up my fork, trying to squelch the doubts and guilt that suddenly assailed me. This was serious business and I couldn't tell Aunt Lily the whole truth: I was a suspect in Hillman's murder—and part of my desperation about writing the news story is that I was trying to stay out of jail. Ugh. The very word made me cringe.

I stabbed at another piece of mango, but when I popped it into my mouth, it felt like a cold lump that I could barely get down my throat.

Chapter Six

I stayed at Aunt Lily's for another hour, waiting to see if this all-knowing, all-snooping handyman, Sam, would return her call. He didn't. She told me not to worry, that he would get back to her within the day. In the meantime, she called three quilters, one notably named Sally Burton, who drove the lone island taxi and was apparently privy to every tidbit of information that moved on the island. All of them agreed to put out an all-points bulletin to track down Sam.

I have to say, my spirits revived a little at the considerable number of draftees my great aunt was able to summon in sixty minutes. Maybe I wasn't really alone like I thought. People who didn't even know me volunteered their services.

I hugged her in gratitude, gave Biscuits and Gravy a quick pet, and drove back to the *Observer* office.

Luckily, Anita sat ensconced in her office, reading afternoon news briefs from the AP, and Sandy was occupied on the telephone with one of the island marinas that wanted to buy advertising space for an upcoming fishing tournament.

Hooray. I could actually have time to myself to finish my story.

I laid claim to the computer and brought up my nearly finished story on Hillman's murder. Reading through it, I gave myself a mental pat on the back. It wasn't half bad. Of course, Anita would hack it to smithereens, but my writing seemed to be improving. To my untrained eye.

After two more hours, I polished it off and set a hard copy on Anita's desk. I made another copy and faxed it over to Chrissy at the Starfish Lodge for our critique session tomorrow morning. Hooray, again. I'd actually made my Friday deadline.

"How does it feel to have written your first hard news story?" Anita asked.

"Okay." My eyes riveted on the inch-long ash hanging from the cigarette between her lips. "I didn't get the chance to add the new info I found about Hillman's 'good deeds.' I need to verify the sources."

"Spoken like a true reporter." Her cigarette bobbed, causing the ash to dangle precariously. "Save it for the next story—this murder spells out at least a three-week series."

Great. "Have you heard anything about Hillman sponsoring a Little Brother named Todd Griffith?"

"Nope. And I'm not sure I believe it. Make certain you double check the sources."

"Maybe Hillman had a soft side for kids."

"And I'm going to become a trapeze artist for the Ringling circus." She laughed as she finally tapped her cigarette in the shriveled potted plant next to her desk. "This story is just the beginning. You'll be ready for the *Detroit Free Press* by the time I'm done with you."

"As long as I stay out of jail." Or Soft Haven—that was the mental institution located about twenty miles away on the mainland. I'd been tempted ever since I took the reporting job at the *Observer* to see if my predecessor ended up there. No one would tell me what happened to her, except that she left to pick up lunch at the island Dairy Queen one day and never came back. I feared the worst—she went berserk in the drive-thru after finding out her cheeseburger was minus lettuce, pickle, and mustard—but I didn't have the nerve to find out for sure.

"You're not still worried about Detective Billie, are you?"

"No . . . well, maybe a little."

"I'll take care of him."

"Thanks."

Anita held up the hard copy of my news story. "And this too." She winked.

I ducked out before she could get started on her usual editorial slice and dice.

Most of all, I needed to put Hillman's murder out of my mind, for a little while at least.

I waved to Sandy who was gathering up her iPod and magazines. "Have a good weekend."

"You too." I exited before Anita could nab me. I was outta there. Freedom.

I drove toward the Twin Palms RV Resort, noticing the clouds gathered off to the west of Mango Bay. They weren't the usual puffy white concoctions that drifted in from the Gulf of Mexico during the evening. These clouds appeared like bloated gray balloons, dark and threatening. And not moving. Just lingering off in the distance. An uneasy twinge pulled at my tummy.

As I pulled into my spot next to the Airstream, I noticed my honeymooning neighbors were still no where to be seen, although two swimsuits were now clothespinned to their awning: a metallic gold string bikini and a pair of matching gold satin men's swim trunks. Sexy. Provocative. Hot. At least they were still alive and apparently had enough physical energy left over from their connubial exertions to swim.

As I climbed out of Rusty, that uneasy feeling returned. Something was off-kilter.

I glanced around my RV site. Nothing looked amiss. But as I moved toward my Airstream, the feeling grew into a wave of apprehension that swept through me. Stark and vivid. My palms began to sweat, my heart beat a little faster. What was wrong?

Then I saw it.

I gasped and covered my mouth so I wouldn't scream.

A large, white egret was lying dead across my picnic table.

After a few moments of complete immobilization, I stumbled into my Airstream, grabbed Kong, and called Wanda Sue. I don't know what I said, but she arrived within minutes.

"Mallie, what's going on? Are you okay?" She banged on the Airstream screen door.

Cautiously, I emerged and pointed at the picnic table.

"Oh, my goodness." She grimaced.

"Is it . . . uh . . . dead?" I swallowed hard. These words echoed with distressing familiarity. At least this time, it was only a bird.

"I think so." She prodded the limp, still form.

"But how? . . . I mean, could it have had a heart attack or stroke or something? Do birds have those kinds of things happen to them?" I knew the answer but, for some reason, unless Wanda Sue actually said it, I could pretend that it wasn't true.

"Nah. Looks like it was shot."

There went that illusion. "A practical joke?"

"Not likely." Her face looked grim—or at least as somber as Wanda Sue's sunny features could appear. The bright pink tube top and flowered Capri pants didn't help much either.

"That means . . . someone must've killed it and put it

on my picnic table," I said the words slowly, hesitantly. "But why?"

Wanda Sue transferred her gaze to me. "Can't say, honey."

A cold knot formed in my stomach. "What should we do with it?" I mumbled.

"I'll call Pop Pop Welch at maintenance. He'll know what to do." She disappeared inside the Airstream. While she was in there, I clutched Kong to my chest and avoided looking at the dead egret.

Wanda Sue came out again. "Pop Pop said he'd be here ASAP."

Half an hour later, a golf cart slowly rolled up, Pop Pop Welch at the wheel. Eighty if he were a day, Pop Pop had two arthritic knees, a heart condition, and cataracts. He shuffled toward the picnic table, mumbling to himself on the way.

"What do you think?" Wanda Sue asked.

Pop Pop lifted a wing. It flopped down. "Deader than a doornail." He produced a newspaper from his back pocket and scooped up the bird. "Let's take it to the office and we'll call animal control to dispose of it."

Wanda Sue nodded. Then she turned to me. "I'll be back in a jiffy. You hang in there."

The two of them revved off in the golf cart, leaving Kong and me standing there in the growing darkness. I looked out over the Gulf and saw only a thin yellow line where the sun had set. I shivered.

"Kong, let's hook up the Airstream and get the heck out of here—put a thousand miles between us and this stupid island." He licked my face.

I need to get out of here. Run far, far away. The freedom of the road beckoned. I'd been going south for the last five years, and now I could start moving west. A whole part of the country stretched out there just waiting to be discovered.

"I can't—even if I wanted to." I sighed and buried my face in Kong's soft fur. "Detective Billie said I couldn't leave the area till the case was solved." Why was I speaking to my dog?

Get a grip. I parked him and myself on one of the lounge chairs outside my Airstream, facing out toward the Gulf. The breeze had settled into a soft whisper. Waves rolled in, moving over the sand with barely a murmur. But off to the west, clouds still blackened the sky like a deadly mask ready to reveal itself when the time was right.

Maybe when the mask was stripped away, the sky would open up with a torrent of rain. Or maybe not. I had no way of knowing.

It was safe to say that the dead bird wasn't a joke—no one I'd met on the island thus far had a sense of humor that twisted, except maybe Anita. She had Charles Addams' cartoons pinned to the bulletin board in her office, and seemed particularly fond of the one where a man in a car was fiendishly encouraging another driver to pass him on a blind curve as an oncoming truck, in the opposite lane, barreled toward the poor, unsuspecting driver. Funny. Real funny.

Depraved humor aside, I couldn't quite see Anita killing a bird for fun. For a pack of cigarettes maybe, but she didn't seem in short supply of them.

No, the dead bird was a warning. The murderer was warning me to back off the case.

Okay, take stock of the situation, I told myself. I couldn't run, and there was no place to hide. Sure, the old Mallie would've hit the road and not looked back. But something had happened to me the last few days and I knew I couldn't do that. The only way to handle this situation was head on. I had to be strong.

I closed my eyes and took a few calming breaths, wishing I knew how to do Sandy's TM.

Just then, Kong let out a couple of short, loud barks. My eyes snapped open. I turned around and saw Wanda Sue's familiar mile-high beehive hair approaching.

"You okay?"

"I . . . I think so."

"Should we call Detective Billie?" She strolled toward Kong and me, and he responded by growling low in his throat. I whispered soothing words into his ears and he stopped.

"No." If I told him what happened, that would be the end of my involvement in the murder case. He wouldn't give me so much as a one-line press release. And it's possible he wouldn't believe me anyway. He didn't trust me. Hell, he hardly knew me.

Wanda Sue hesitated. "All right. But if anything else happens, *I'm* calling him." She sat down in the lounge chair next to me.

The outside lights of my neighbors' million-dollar motorhome flipped on.

I eyed the gorgeous, sleek testament to RV technology. "I don't suppose they saw anything."

"The Clarks? Ha."

"Is that their name?" Needless to say, I still didn't know what they looked like. "They've never come out of their RV."

"Honeymooners." Wanda Sue's laughter rang out in a light, feminine trill. One of those Southern laughs that ran a full scale and then some. It felt sort of nice—like balm on my spirits after the recent trauma.

"Lucky them." I pushed the image of the dead egret out of my mind.

Silence descended on us as we watched those looming clouds off in the gulf.

"I heard that Everett went whining and complaining to Nick Billie about you." She gave an exclamation of disgust. "That old man is meaner than a snake and uglier than a porcupine."

I sat up slowly. "Just how mean do you think he is?"

She imitated my movement. "Honey, I see where you're going. And if you ask me, he's capable of killing man or bird. Yessiree." She dragged out the last word as if it were the last note in an aria. "He once elbowed a man at Whiteside's who picked up the last tin of Mabel's favorite cat food, and he used a BB gun to shoot some bunnies that were eating on his hibiscus bushes. Can you imagine that?"

"He could kill a bird—especially if he'd thought it would scare me." My mind began to race. "He told me that he had some kind running feud with Hillman about the boundary line between their properties. Not to mention Mabel."

"His cat?" She exhaled loudly. "Now I love my own precious little kitty—Riley—love him to pieces. But he ain't a person. Old Everett treats that creature like a feline princess. If you ask me, that's plum unhealthy."

Kong barked in agreement. I agreed with his agreement.

"Are you sure you don't want to talk to Detective Billie about that dead bird?"

"I'm sure."

"If that's what you want to do, I'll go along with it." She leaned over and gave me a brief hug. "But you need to be careful."

She was right. Whoever killed that bird, whether it was Everett or not, didn't like the fact that I was writing stories about Hillman's murder. *And now he's watching me.*

Oh, goody.

We sat there a good long time, without speaking. The sky suddenly seemed to grow even darker.

The next morning, I awoke to the sound of tapping on the side of my Airstream. I moaned. It had been a long, restless night and I didn't feel like getting up.

The tapping continued. Kong opened his eyes from where he lay on my pillow and began yapping. We both staggered toward the door and I peeped out the window.

Outside was an older man with teak-colored skin and a mostly bald head, sporting a gold stud in his left ear. He wore a black T-shirt with the word "enigma" splashed across the front and a pair of jeans. In spite of the casual dress and the earring, he looked like an aging professor—scruffy, yet scholarly.

"Who is it?" I asked, straightening my poodle pajama top and matching pants.

"Sam. I'm a friend of your Aunt Lily's."

I exhaled in relief and swung open the door. Kong stationed himself between my feet and treated the intruder with his most menacing growl. Of course, the sound would hardly strike terror in the heart of anyone without a pacemaker and triple by-pass, but Kong did his best to protect me.

"Hi, I'm Mallie."

"Nice to meet you. Lily's told me a lot about you." He held up a box of donuts.

A slow smile spread across my face. "I can see that."

"She's a lady of inestimable talents . . ." He pulled out two styrofoam cups from a white paper bag.

I inhaled in delight. Coffee. Lovely, black coffee. The wonderful aroma filled the air and drew me toward it as if it were a java magnet and I was a polarized, caffeine-starved zombie.

"How about we sit out here and enjoy the sunrise?" Sam set the box on my red-checkered-cloth-covered picnic table.

"Lovely." I scanned the horizon to the east and noticed the sun had risen a fair distance in the sky already. I wish I could've completely blamed the restless night, but the truth is I've always been a late riser. Those people who are up with the birds, chipper and singing at dawn, always struck me as slightly demented.

"How long have you known my great aunt?" I took a deep swallow of my coffee and let it flow through my veins. Wonderful. The sleep fog began to clear from my mind. I seated myself on the picnic table bench.

"Nearly twenty-five years." He seated himself across from me. "I drifted around a bit after Vietnam and, eventually, found myself on Coral Island without a job, little money, and a drinking problem."

"Oh." What else could I say? Sam certainly didn't waste any time hiding behind platitudes and nice aphorisms.

"Lily was the only person who'd give me job—if I got off the addiction to adult beverages. She's like that. Kind. But tough in the right sort of way."

"I know." I bit into my first donut of the day. Crispy on the outside, all soft and squishy on the inside. Yum.

"And when she loves you, it's forever," Sam added.

I stopped chewing. What was he saying?

He laughed. "It's not like that. Lily's affections were engaged elsewhere. We're friends. But sometimes that's an even deeper relationship."

I started chewing again. I knew how much Aunt Lily loved Uncle Benjamin—he died in the Korean War, and she never married again. I'd always thought it was incredibly romantic that she loved only one man her whole life. So different from my own superficial, light-hearted, hit-and-run relationships.

I took another swig of coffee. "I guess she told you I'm doing a series of stories on Jack Hillman—"

"And that you found his body." His eyes searched my face. Light gray searchlights peering into my soul. I lowered my eyes.

"Yeah." I peered into the dark liquid inside my coffee cup. "It was . . . horrible." Images of the body flashed through my mind again. The blood. The unseeing eyes. The knife.

"I can imagine." His voice was quiet.

Reaching for another donut, I cleared my head. "I really shouldn't have two, but I can't resist."

Sam sipped his coffee and merely smiled.

"Anyway, I'm writing these stories on Hillman and getting conflicting information."

"Few people are one-dimensional," Sam commented.

"True."

"Including you."

I gave a short, self-deprecating laugh. "I'm pretty much a what-you-see-is-what-you-get kind of girl."

"I doubt that."

"I usually take things as they come and not give 'em a second thought." *Until I became a murder suspect.*

Sam focused a direct glance on me again. "Maybe you've changed."

"Maybe." I didn't want to think about that.

"How can I help you?"

"Aunt Lily told me you were 'the man'."

He laughed. "Because I'm so wise?"

"Not exactly."

"Because I've see death in the war?"

"Not really."

His brows rose.

"It's because you're in everybody's house fixing things—"

"Snooping around?"

I grinned.

He grinned back. "I never snoop. But I can't deny that people tell me things that they wouldn't reveal to their closest friends. It makes sense. I'm in their house, seeing the private details of their lives. Handymen are like bartenders—we're a receptive audience often to lonely people, and we need their . . . patronage."

"Did you ever do any work for Hillman?"

"Only a plumbing job—and he was out of town."

"Darn." I sighed. "You know, Hillman was a real jerk the day I met him, but I've come to see that he wasn't like that all the time. He did some good things in his life too. And nobody seems to know or even care—"

"And you think delving into the 'real' Hillman will lead you to the murderer."

"Well . . . yes."

"For your newspaper?"

I nodded, crossing my fingers under the table at telling the partial lie. Or at least not giving him the whole truth that I was also a suspect.

Sam's hands wrapped around his coffee cup. He was of medium height, with a stocky build—kinda like a bulldog. But his hands were those of a poet with long fingers and slender palms. "If you want to know why Hillman was murdered, you need to find out what he was hiding from the world."

"Like his sponsoring a Little Brother?"

"Yes."

"But why would he hide something like that? Wouldn't he want people to know that he had a soft side?"

"Not necessarily. Everyone has something in his past that he wouldn't want other people to know."

"Even you?"

"Especially me."

I stared at Sam for a few moments and found nothing but gentle contemplation in his gray eyes.

"Dig deep enough, and you'll find out why he was

murdered. Just be careful. Whoever killed him could be a model citizen also hiding something."

"Light and dark?"

"Of course . . . we're all a mixture of the divine and the diabolical."

Even me? Mixed-up Mallie? Was I hiding part of myself? I wasn't sure that I wanted to know the answer to that question.

Chapter Seven

Sam stayed for a little while longer—enough time for me to have nibbled on yet another donut and finished off my coffee. He promised to get back with me before the weekend was over.

Then, he drove off in his ancient Volvo—a 240 which hasn't been in production for over twenty years. It had that lumbering turtle-like quality Volvo used to have before they decided to get competitive with upscale import vehicles. Solid. Dependable. With a backseat full of power tools.

He'd given me a lot to think about . . . more than I usually thought about anything. And I wasn't certain I was ready to change from Mixed-up Mallie to Deep-Thinking Mallie. Frankly, I wasn't sure I had it in me.

I walked Kong, showered, and put on my favorite

blue jean sundress. It had spaghetti straps and ended just above the knee. Perfect for the Florida heat. Even better, it had good vibes because I wore the dress on the day I quit working at Disney World.

As I climbed into Rusty, I reached for my new sunblock with SPF forty-five, but realized my sunburned, peeling nose might not need it after all. The clouds had moved in from the west and now covered the sky like a slate-colored blanket of dust and grime. Churning up shadows and waiting to empty its pouches of rain.

Brushing the damp curls from my forehead, I rolled down the window of my truck. It might not be sunny, but it sure as heck was humid—maybe even more so than when the sunlight dried everything out.

I drove to the Starfish Lodge and parked right in front of one of the big windows, just in time to see Everett and Bradley deep in conversation right outside the Lodge's entrance. Everett was gesturing wildly with his hands, then threw them up and stalked off. Bradley watched him leave and followed soon after.

Hardly surprising.

As I entered the Lodge, I spotted the group at their usual table. The dining room contained only one other couple—a middle-aged man and his wife wearing those STUPID and I'M WITH STUPID T-shirts. Enough said.

Mercifully, quiet reigned in the dining room this morning.

"Mallie, come on over," Chrissy exclaimed. She wore

a camouflage-print tank dress and was seated next to George.

"How is everyone today?" I asked.

"Betty and I are doing pretty good." Burt refilled his margarita glass. My eyes widened at the sight of the half-empty pitcher this early in the morning.

"It's non-alcoholic, honey," Betty said to me, handing her empty glass to her husband.

"I'm okay . . . I guess, considering I'm still in s . . . shock over Jack's death," George said, with just a trace of a stammer. His hair was brushed back, so I got a good look at his face. Not bad, I thought. Clear hazel eyes in a sensitive, finely chiseled face. His mouth was drawn in a tight line, though, as if suppressing strong emotion.

"How about you, Chrissy?" I said.

"Hanging in there." She sighed. "We all still miss Jack."

Yeah, and pigs fly, I wanted to say.

"Our critiquing isn't nearly as good as it was when Jack gave us direction," she continued.

Before I could respond, a waitress appeared and placed a glass of water in front of me, inquiring if I wanted breakfast. I shook my head. After already downing three mouthwatering, vein-clogging donuts, I decided to stick with the water.

I dropped my canvas bag on the floor with a distinct thud. "I thought all of you were upset over how he verbally assaulted your work—I know I was."

"Yeah, but we learned from it." Chrissy twisted a lock of her long, blond hair around her index finger. "I'm not saying that Jack couldn't get outta line at times, but I really was growing as a writer. And if I want to eventually publish from my blog, I need to write the best poetry that I can."

"Uh-huh," Burt and Betty echoed their agreement.

"I think more positive feedback is a better way of critiquing." I sat down next to George. A strong, musky-scented aftershave emanated from him. The kind that was supposed to make you think of piney woods on an autumn day, but really conjured up images of dried tree bark and rotten leaves. I inched my chair away from him.

"But Jack obviously helped you," Chrissy said.

"What do you mean?" I asked.

She held up the copy of my article that I'd faxed over to the Lodge last night. "We thought this piece was loads better than your last one."

"Absolutely," Burt chimed in.

"It's a g . . . great improvement," George added.

"Really?" I glanced around the table in surprise. Everyone nodded. "Maybe it's the subject matter. A murder makes a much more interesting story than a disputed bike path."

"True, but it's not just that." Burt took the story from Chrissy and paged through it. "The sentences are much crisper . . . no passive voice. Lots of human interest. Your voice is coming through."

Betty lifted the story from her husband's grasp. "I

particularly liked the section about Jack's life. You get a feel for who he was. It made you want to know him."

I listened in dazed delight as they went on complimenting my story. I probably should've stopped them when the words, "Pulitzer Prize," began to be bandied about, but hey, it isn't everyday that a girl gets to hear something like that.

"So you see, Jack did help you to become a better writer in only one session," Chrissy wound up the group's effusive panegyrics.

"I guess you're right," I admitted. Maybe they were right, but I still didn't wholeheartedly agree with Jack's methods.

"Here's to Jack." Burt held up his margarita glass.

We all raised our glasses. "To Jack," we echoed.

After our toast, Burt and Betty passed around a short story they'd been working on: a western about two men, a woman, and a horse. I wasn't sure if the men were fighting over the woman or the horse, but the descriptions of the desert were rather pretty. We critiqued them for about twenty minutes, then decided to take a break. When Chrissy excused herself, I waited a discreet interval and then followed her into the women's restroom. Actually, the sign on the door said GULLS and the men's room, not to be outdone, sported a BUOYS plaque. The Starfish Lodge took its nautical décor seriously.

When I entered, my fellow gull was fluffing her long blond hair in the mirror.

"Just needed to wash my hands," I said, moving toward the sink.

Chrissy smiled. She finished with her hair and began to trace the lines of her mouth with a tinted, all-natural lip pencil. Then she applied her coordinating lipstick—one of those not-tested-on-animals brands that you buy in expensive health food stores.

I glanced at my own pale, uncolored lips. I would've produced my lipstick, but it was a three-fifty cheapie full of unhealthy artificial dyes, and I didn't want to hear a lecture.

"Chrissy, if you don't mind my asking, what was your relationship with Jack?"

She paused ever so slightly in her lip ministrations. "Off the record?"

I nodded.

"Kiss and cuddle. Great while it lasted, but neither of us thought it would lead to anything permanent. I'm a vegan—he ate meat at every meal." She shuddered visibly. "Besides, that hard-bitten, hard-nosed, in-your-face writer routine got a little old, you know what I mean?"

"You bet." I took the opportunity to jump in. "But there was more to him than all that macho stuff. While I was doing research on Jack's life, I found out he belonged to Big Brothers/Big Sisters and donated big time to the Island Museum."

She tossed the lip pencil and lipstick into her purse.

"I don't know anything about the museum, but the thing with the kids doesn't surprise me. He liked 'em."

"He did?"

"Oh, yeah. I know it's hard to believe, but he told me he wanted to start a creative writing camp for kids—just couldn't afford to do it until next summer."

"But I thought his books sold well."

"They *did*, but he hadn't published anything new except a couple of short stories in four or five years."

I locked eyes with her in the mirror. "You mean Jack was experiencing . . . writer's block?"

"He liked to call it a 'creative pothole,' but it was writer's block all right. I don't know what caused it—maybe all that meat—but he hadn't been able to come up with a new book idea since *Men on Death Row.*"

"That could also explain why he was doing the Writers' Institutes—to make money."

"He had a lot of expenses—the sailboat, the sporty car, the upkeep on his house. It all added up."

"Was he still getting royalties on previous books?"

"I'm not sure. If he did, it wasn't very much." She gave her hair another fluff and slipped the purse strap over her shoulder.

"One last thing, what do you know about Burt and Betty aside from their penchant for margaritas?"

"Not much. They've got a small ranch outside Tucumcari, and they've just about finished their collection of short stories. Burt likes horses, Betty likes to cook.

They don't have any kids, but he has an elderly mother who's in a nursing home in Albuquerque."

My eyes widened in respect. "I'd say you've gleaned quite a bit about them."

"I listen—that's the key. Most people talk so much, they never take the time to really listen to what others have to say."

Ouch. Put me in that category with my motor mouth. But I was learning to put my engine in idle—at least some of the time.

"I also have the feeling that they attended one of Jack's Institutes before."

"Why's that?"

"Just the way they seemed to know his working patterns—they clued George and me in on them right at the beginning. Burt also taped the critique sessions, which I thought was odd. He said it was so he could play it back and learn even more, but I didn't buy that. He was taping for another reason."

"Such as?" I prompted.

"I don't know. Maybe they didn't trust Jack. Or maybe they were a bit paranoid. Writers can be like that sometimes."

"Even George?"

A dreamy smile appeared on her face. "No, he's a prince."

Shy, stuttering George? My, he had made some major headway with her in a short time. Maybe that was all part of his plan. Get Hillman out of the way and move in on Chrissy.

She took one last look in the mirror and gave me a wink. Then she breezed out.

I stood there a few minutes, contemplating what she'd said. She and Hillman had been close—no surprise there. And no motive to kill him—unless it was revenge at having had to see him bare-chested in the hottub. Reason enough, but not a real motive.

I was more interested in her revelation that Hillman had financial problems. It opened up a whole world of possibilities. He might've been engaged in illegal activities, such as drug smuggling or goodness knows what. The ten thousand islands were only two hours away and that area was a nest for all kinds of nasty shenanigans, from Florida panther poaching to gun running.

And where did Burt and Betty fit in? If they didn't trust Jack, why did they take another Writers' Institute with him? That didn't add up. Unless they attended just for an excuse to guzzle down the margaritas.

And George? Was he a "prince" or a jealous murderer? Had he wanted Chrissy bad enough that he was willing to get rid of Hillman—permanently?

The questions hammered at my brain as I tried to piece together the puzzle. But no answers presented themselves. I splashed a little water on my face and, for good measure, fluffed up my own hair. I might not possess Chrissy's gleaming golden tresses, but my red curls weren't too shabby. I dabbed more sunblock on my peeling nose and slathered an extra layer on my freckled arms. I'd never have that healthy glow like Chrissy, but at least I could prevent my skin from looking like a boiled lobster.

I left the restroom and returned to the table. As I approached, George said, "M . . . Mallie, we decided that we're like that group of writers who called themselves the 'Round Table' at the Alg . . . gon—"

"Algonquin," Burt cut in.

"The writers who met in New York City during the thirties?" I asked.

"Yep." George beamed. "We're like them."

I scanned the table, imagining Betty as Dorothy Parker—she certainly shared Parker's affinity for booze, if not the same razor-sharp wit. But who would that make Burt? Chrissy? I couldn't remember who the other writers were at the Algonquin, but none of them struck me as clones of our Coral Island group.

"How long are you going to continue to meet?" I seated myself across from George.

"I'm not sure," Betty chimed in. "We have to stay on the island till we're cleared as suspects—detective's orders," Betty supplied.

"He indicated that it probably wouldn't take all that long," Burt added, "since we all have alibis."

"You never know." George was gazing at Chrissy with the same adoration Kong lavished on me when he received one of his gourmet doggie treats.

"True." I sipped my water, keeping a few chips of ice to chew on. It was a bad habit and the reason why I had six crowns on my molars, but I loved the sensation of crunching on hard, frozen water. "Burt, I noticed you didn't tape today's critique session. Don't you usually tape them?"

"Uh . . . no. Well . . . yes, I did tape them when Jack was presiding. But now that it's just us, I decided to dispense with the recorder."

Betty said nothing.

"Sometimes I'd forget Jack's exact comments. The tape recorder helped because I could play it back later and listen to his suggestions a couple more times." Burt avoided my eyes. He was hiding something. I could feel it.

"Really?" I couldn't resist lowering my brows in disapproval. "I'd walk through a patch of prickly pear cactus barefoot before I'll listen to the tape of Hillman trashing my writing. Even if it helped my articles. I think there are nicer ways to make a person a better writer."

No one responded.

"I think it's time to hear my new works." Chrissy opened the poetry portfolio from her blog. "This is one of my "Inspiration through Nature" poems." She cleared her throat and began in a singsong voice,

Through all life's little ups and downs
Especially when you're going through chemo,

*Remember that vitamins and minerals abound
And they'll soon have you feeling so primo.*

Huh? There were a few more stanzas, but I think I blocked them out. Keats she was not.

"What do you think?" she asked the group when she finished. "The poems each target a certain disease and how natural cures can help. That one was for people who've contracted cancer. I've also got ones for diabetes, stroke, ulcers, and heart attacks."

"Wonderful!" George enthused.

"Charming." Burt clapped.

"Lovely," Betty added.

Gag me. I had to make a quick exit before she started reading inappropriately upbeat verse for stroke victims. "I've gotta go . . . sorry." I stood up and grabbed my canvas bag. "Thanks for the critique."

"When's your story going to be in the paper?" Burt asked.

"The edition comes out on Tuesday."

"What about your next one?" George asked.

"I'll start on it this week—"

"Don't forget to bring it by for critiquing," Chrissy reminded me.

"I won't." I pivoted and moved away from the table.

"Oh, Mallie, I forgot to tell you," Burt brought me up short. "While you were in the restroom, some guy named Sam stopped by. He said he had some information for you."

I turned around. "Did he say what?"

"Nope," Burt said. "Said he'd get it to you later."

"Oh." Darn. Another lead shot down. "Thanks anyway."

As I moved toward the lobby, I caught snatches of Chrissy's poem:

Not to worry if you can't get around,
With a little enzyme therapy,
You'll be feeling safe and sound.

Ohmygosh.

When I reached Rusty, I spied a note clipped to the only working windshield wiper.

Slowly, I unfolded the sheet.

Talk to Nora Cresswell at the Seafood Shanty.

Sam. Thank goodness. He'd taken the time to write out his message for me. I had a new lead after all.

Chapter Eight

I drove to the police station first. I still had to drop off the transcript of my statement. When I walked in, the receptionist told me Detective Billie would be back in a few minutes, but I said I couldn't wait. I wanted to get on the road to the Seafood Shanty as quickly as possible so I could mull over the morning's revelations about Hillman.

"But Nick said he wanted to talk to you," she protested.

"I'll stop by later. See ya."

I exited before she could say anything else and quickly drove off.

As Rusty lurched along, I realized that Anita had been right when she told me to "follow the money." If Hillman had writer's block for several years, he was probably financially strapped—a situation not unknown to me.

That explained the Writers' Institute. He recruited aspiring authors of varying talents (or lack thereof) and relieved them of their savings on the promise he could get them published. It was a quick way to earn some cash. And maybe only the tip of the iceberg. *Who knows what else he was up to?*

Illegal drugs? That was usually the answer for someone living on a Florida island who appeared to be making money without any gainful employment. And Anita had told me when I first arrived on Coral Island that the *Observer* had run a lot of local drug-trafficking stories the previous year. Nothing with Hillman that I could remember, but that might only mean he hadn't been caught—yet. It was a fast way to earn big amounts of money—and sometimes a quick trip to that giant Airstream in the sky. At least that was my vision of heaven. A brand-new, fully loaded, gleaming silver Airstream with wings.

A car horn blared behind me. I was jolted out of my reverie and noticed Rusty was barely tipping thirty-five miles per hour. I rammed down the pedal, knowing my truck's maximum speed barely topped fifty.

I'd never been to the Seafood Shanty before. Located on the road that led off the island, it was a hangout for local fishermen and bikers—kind of a seedy place. The owner had painted FAMILY RESTAURANT boldly across one side of the building, but I don't think it fooled anyone. The motorcycles parked in front told the real story.

As I approached the place, I noted it looked run

down. A long, low building with a sagging roof, it boasted a ramshackle front porch, torn screens, and peeling paint. At least Rusty would look right at home parked in front of the place.

I made for the front porch, carefully stepping around the holes in the floorboards. As I entered, I realized the inside was just as run down as the outside—same peeling paint and uneven floor. Assorted fishing nets were strung across the ceiling—presumably for decoration—and a large anchor hung on the wall behind the bar.

About half a dozen men were seated at the bar, and two biker couples occupied a table toward the back of the room. Otherwise, the place was quiet. Except for the country western music that played in the background. Not being a fan of that kind of music, I couldn't tell who was singing—except that it was a man with a twangy voice. That probably narrowed the field to under a hundred.

Several large paddle fans whirled overhead, which was a good thing. The Seafood Shanty wasn't air-conditioned, and I was already feeling the heat. I dreaded to think what the kitchen looked or smelled like.

I sat down at a small table toward the side of the building where dirty screens offered the possibility of a breeze.

After a few moments, a young woman in shorts and a tank top approached. She had dyed blond hair swept up in a messy ponytail. The color had grown out, and dark brown roots showed near the scalp. Her face, though

unlined, already had that haggard look of someone who
worked long hours for little pay. And the flat look in her
eyes said she knew her life wasn't going to get better
any time soon.

"What can I do ya for?" She slid a pencil out from
behind her ear and held it poised above her order pad.

"Does Nora Cresswell work here?"

"Yeah."

"Is she here today?"

"Yeah."

"Could I speak with her?" I persisted.

She fastened a hard look in my direction. "You're
talking to her. What do you want?"

"Just a few minutes of your time."

"No, I meant what do you want to drink?"

"Uh . . . iced tea?"

She exhaled impatiently. "Look, honey, this is a bar
and we serve booze here. What do want?"

"A beer?" I inquired. "I'm not sure what brand—"

"You got it." Scribbling a few words on her order
pad, she turned away.

"Could I talk to you?"

She was already gone. Damn. It might be difficult to
get Nora to open up to a total stranger. But I didn't have
a motor mouth for nothing.

By the time she returned with my beer, I was ready.

"Thanks so much. It's incredibly hot today, isn't it? I
couldn't believe the heat and humidity when I left Mango
Bay—a cloudy morning and it was already hitting around

eighty-five degrees. And it wasn't even ten o'clock. I can only imagine what it's going to be like this summer. Just hot, hot, and more hot."

"Hot," she echoed in a bored tone.

I reached into my canvas bag and rooted around until I found a pack of gum. "Care for spearmint? It's cooling." I held out a piece.

"I don't mind if I do. Thanks." She popped it in her mouth and began to chew.

"Have you lived here long, Nora?" I summoned what I hoped appeared to be an inviting smile.

"Long enough." She placed one hand on her hip, still bored.

"I guess you know just about everybody on the island then."

"Pretty near."

"What about Jack Hillman? Did you know him?"

She stopped chewing, her interest sparking. "What's this all about?" her voice hardened.

"Okay, I'll give it to you straight. I'm Mallie Monroe and I work for the *Observer*. I've started writing a series of articles about Hillman's murder—"

"I don't know nothing about that."

"I heard that you . . . uh . . . knew him."

"He came in here and had a couple drinks every so often. We were friends. That's all."

"Did he ever talk to you?"

"Sure. He had to give me his orders." She started

chewing her gum again with rapid, jerking motions of her jaw.

"Did he mention that he had any enemies?"

"No." Her features shuttered down.

"I don't mean to upset you. I just wanted to know—"

"If he and I had an affair? Go ahead—say it. Everyone on the island thinks it, but they're wrong. I never cheated on my husband. Never." She thumped the table with her hand.

The bikers glanced in our direction.

"Nora, take it easy. I believe you."

"Really?" Surprise laced through her voice.

"Yeah . . . I do."

"Well . . . you're probably the only person who does."

"I know what it feels like to be gossiped about. Not on Coral Island, but in the Midwest where I was raised. My family just couldn't comprehend why I didn't want to settle into a career, get married, and have kids—all in that order. They whispered behind my back at times—just because they didn't understand me." I paused, crossing my fingers at the lie. A lot of it was true. "I'm not asking you about Hillman just because I'm writing the story. *I* was the one who found his body—"

"Oh, no. How awful for you." She slumped into the chair next to me and dropped her head in her hands. "I just can't believe he's dead . . . it's so horrible. To think that someone could've killed him like that."

"I know." Memories of the body came surging up in my mind like water spewing up from an underground well. Dark, deep, and hidden. I could see him dead at his desk as though he were in front of me right now—head flung back, blood stains on his shirt. *Don't think about it.*

"Most people thought Jack was a real jerkface . . . even my own husband, Pete."

"Did he, too, suspect you and Hillman had an affair?" I asked gently.

She turned her face up, her eyes tear-stained. "Yeah. But it wasn't true, I swear it. Pete was in jail, and I was lonely . . . All Jack and I did was go out a few times and talk. Nothing more."

"And the next thing you know is you're being branded a scarlet woman?"

"Huh?"

"Nothing." Nix the Hawthorne reference.

"When Pete got out of jail, some of his so-called buddies couldn't wait to tell him that I'd been carrying on with Jack. Pete was furious. He's always been such a sweet guy, but when he heard about me and Jack, he went berserk. Swore he'd get back at Jack if it was the last thing he'd do."

"When was that?"

"About a month ago." She wiped the tears away with the back of her hand. "Pete hasn't spoken to me since."

"Nora, do you think he could've . . . murdered Hillman? Was he that angry?"

She dropped her eyes to the floor.

"Nora?"

"I . . . I don't know," she whispered. "To tell you the truth, I've been afraid even to think about it."

"Did Detective Billie question you yet?"

"No, but I'm expecting him any day. I don't know what I'm going to say."

"The truth . . . it's always best." I patted her hand. "Do you know where Pete is?"

"He hangs out at the Trade Winds Marina with some of the other fishermen. They're okay guys. But sometimes I think they sit around and talk too much about old times. The fishing industry isn't what it used to be since the net ban. Fishermen who'd cast nets for generations couldn't fish with them anymore, but a lot of the guys did it on the side. Pete's their hero because he went to jail and refused to rat out the guys who worked for him." A touch of admiration lit her voice.

"I see."

"I'm not saying he did the right thing, but he took his punishment like a man."

"Have you told Pete that you're still in love with him?"

Her mouth trembled. "It shows, huh?"

"Like a beacon."

"I haven't told him. What's the point?" She sniffed and blinked back a fresh flow of tears. "I don't think our relationship has a snowball's chance of making it, but I still hope . . ."

"You never know." It was lame, I knew. But anyone who worked in a place like the Seafood Shanty needed encouragement. "Did Hillman ever say anything about being short of money?"

"Him?" She looked up, her eyes wide in surprise. "No way. He always tipped big."

"Just curious."

"Now that you mention it, he did say a couple of times that he worried about the high cost of college tuition. I just thought he was making conversation . . . you know, how expensive everything is—that kind of thing."

College tuition? Something clicked in my brain. Of course. I mentally snapped my fingers. If Todd Griffith from Big Brothers/Big Sisters was finishing up high school, he'd be going to college this fall. Hillman needed money for his tuition.

"Is something wrong?" Nora asked. "You look like you swallowed a lemon or something.

"No, I'm fine." I'd compressed my lips so the motor mouth wouldn't kick in and reveal what I thinking.

"I don't really think my husband could've killed Jack," she added.

"That says a lot. You still believe in him."

"I guess I do." A tiny glimmer of optimism brightened her face.

"Nora, baby, we'd like some more drinks over here," a burly biker shouted the other side of the room.

"I've got to go back to work." She rose, brushing

back strays hair with a shaky hand. "Thanks for listening—and the gum."

"Anytime."

As she made her way toward the biker group, I tossed a few dollars on the table for the beer and added a generous tip. If anyone could use a break, it was Nora.

I emerged from the Seafood Shanty as if I were coming out from under a cloud into the sunlight. Speaking of clouds . . . I looked up. Still overcast, the sky looked the same. Flat gray clouds hovered low, and not a hint of breeze stirred the heavy, humid air.

When the rain began, it was going to be a doozy.

I hopped back into Rusty and covered the short distance to the Trade Winds Marina in no time. Located down the road from the Seafood Shanty, the marina separated Coral Island from the mainland, with a tiny fishing village, Paradisio, in between. I'm not sure if the name really reflected this little assortment of fishing shacks and bait shops, but I guess it depends on your point of view. I pulled into the marina and spied a group of fishermen next to the docks stacking rods and reels.

"Hi, have any of you seen Pete?" I asked in my most polite, I'm-just-a-nice-girl tone.

No one looked up, but I thought I heard one or two of them grunt. The group contained men of various ages and stages of sun damage, but all of them wore knee-length white rubber fishing boots. Locals referred to them as "island Reeboks."

"I beg your pardon?"

An old, grizzled-looking man with nut-brown skin and a couple of missing teeth grunted what sounded like, "Smaint fear."

"Huh?" I moved closer. The smell of fish and salt water assailed my senses.

"I said he *ain't here*," the old man enunciated the last two words with slow, careful emphasis.

"Do you know when he'll be back?"

"Nope." He began winding line around a battered fishing reel.

"Would you tell him that Mallie Monroe from the *Observer* wants to talk to him?" I directed my comments to the same old guy. At least he was talking. The other men just ignored me. But I had the sense that they were listening keenly.

He grunted again, focusing on his task.

"I'll take that as a 'yes'." I placed my card on the overturned bucket in front of him where he'd set his fishing knife. "Have him call my phone number at the *Observer*."

"Uh-huh."

I turned around and slammed right into Detective Billie's rock solid chest.

"Oh, sorry, I didn't see you." Breathless, I stepped back. He wore a white short-sleeved shirt and jeans, his dark skin contrasting with the light fabric of his shirt in an intriguing way. Every time I saw him, he was progressively more casual. Perhaps next time in shorts and a muscle shirt? Briefly, images of his wide shoulders and nicely developed arms flitted through my mind and, before I could stop myself, my mouth curved into a smile.

"You look like the cat who's lapped up the cream," he said.

"Actually, I had three donuts this morning."

"It doesn't show." One dark brow lifted as he raked my boyish curves.

"I've got a fast metabolism . . . runs in my family. Everyone on my mother's side can eat and eat and eat and never gain weight. It's absolutely incredible. You wouldn't believe what I can put away in one meal. Appetizer, entrée, dessert—you name it. I can eat—"

"And talk and talk and talk," he quipped.

Several of the fishermen erupted in loud guffaws, and Detective Billie touched my elbow to move me away from them.

"That's another trait from my mother's side—my great aunt, Lily, can talk the stripes off a zebra."

"I know." One side of his mouth twisted upward in an ironic semblance of a smile. "Look, I was driving off the island and saw your truck. Did you get my receptionist's message that I wanted to talk to you?"

"Uh . . . sort of, but I had an urgent errand to run." I guess it was hard to ignore Rusty . . . he was one of a kind.

"At the marina?"

Desperately, I scanned the grounds for some kind of

reason that would've caused my pressing need to be here. I spotted the Paradisio Seafood Market sign. "I needed to buy some . . . shrimp. Yes, some shrimp for dinner tonight. I really like my shrimp fresh and wanted to get it right off the boats, if you know what I mean."

He didn't look as if he was buying it.

"I've gotten spoiled since I came to Coral Island with all the fresh seafood that's available . . . grouper, snook, snapper, not to mention smoked mullet. That's my favorite." Truthfully, I hated smoked anything, but it was a Coral Island specialty and I wanted to show that I knew my seafood.

"Okay, you've made your point," he said wryly.

A boat engine roared into life next to us, causing a cloud of exhaust to spew out.

We both coughed.

"Any new developments on the murder case?" I managed to get out between choking and coughing.

"One or two leads." His dark eyes fastened on me. "What about you? Find out anything you'd care to pass on?"

"Nothing earth-shaking." I licked my suddenly dry lips.

We averted our heads in opposite directions. We were both lying, and we both knew it.

"What about Everett? Dig up anything new on him?" I finally asked. In spite of the morning's revelations, he was still my number one suspect.

"No." His voice was firm, final. *Okay.*

"What did you want to talk to me about?" I finally inquired.

He checked his watch—sleek gold with a brown crocodile strap. Functional elegance. Needless to say, it didn't have a Mickey Mouse figure in the center with tiny white-gloved hands pointing at the hours and minutes. "I don't have time to go into it right now because I've got to see Hillman's attorney about funeral arrangements."

"You?"

"There's nobody else. He wanted to be cremated and have his ashes spread in the Gulf. No ceremony. No fuss."

I tried not to grimace. It sounded so cold. Like the disposal of the dead egret.

"Could you come by the police station tomorrow?"

"On Sunday? Most people take that day off."

"Most people don't have a murder case to solve."

I sighed. "What time do you want me to come by?"

"Late morning." He checked his watch again. "See you then."

"Oh, I dropped the transcript with your receptionist this morning."

"Thanks." He turned and strode toward his truck. Applying my handy-dandy vehicular psychoanalysis, I noted he drove a black, Ford F-150. Cap-covered bed, clean sidewalls, and shiny finish. Wow. A symbol for a man who appeared to have everything under control. That truck could take on anything that the road had to offer.

I looked back at Rusty with his semi-bald tires, dull paint job, and dented front fender. Not pretty by any stretch of the imagination. But he could pull my Airstream and get me where I had to go. That's all I thought a truck needed to do at one time. But now I wondered if maybe I needed more.

For starters, it sure would be nice to have air-conditioning.

Was I becoming a yuppie like my siblings? Next, I'd be trading my sandals for sling-back pumps.

Not likely. I glanced up the road to make certain Detective Billie was out of sight. Then I climbed into Rusty, fired up the engine, and patted him on the dashboard. "Don't worry, old buddy. We're in this together." He backfired a couple of times.

I headed back to the island. Detective Billie would be on the mainland for the afternoon. Hooray. I had free rein to talk to suspects. But who? Pete was out of the question until he contacted me. Burt wasn't a particularly promising possibility. That left Everett. It was time to talk to him again, but now, I knew his weak spot: Mabel.

Chapter Nine

Half an hour later, Rusty lumbered up the shell driveway that led to Everett's house. I honked the horn a couple of times, just to alert him in case he had the urge to aim a BB gun at me. Of course, my horn didn't work much better than anything else on my little truck. Instead of a loud blast, the horn emitted a sound that was somewhere between a high pitched squeak and a tortured groan. Instead of alerting other drivers and pedestrians to my presence, it generally made them look around to see if they had hit an animal or something.

At any rate, my horn didn't alert or alarm Everett. I got no response at all.

I gave a few more pathetic toots.

Finally, I heard a voice yell from inside the house, "I heard you all right, missy."

That was more like it.

"I'd like to talk you," I yelled out from inside my truck.

"We already talked," he shouted back. I could see the outline of his body behind the front screen door.

"I have a little something for Mabel—to make up for my last visit. I know how much she means to you. And being a cat person myself, I wanted her to know that I care." So I was laying it on a bit thick. Food might be the way to a man's stomach, but animals were the way to Everett's sympathies.

"A present?" He cracked open the screen door.

"Yep. A little toy mouse and a catnip ball. Whadaya say? Can I get out of my truck without your calling Nick Billie on me?"

He cackled. "He read you the riot act, huh?"

"Just told me not to annoy you. And I fully intend to live up to my promise. I won't bother you or trespass on your property—unless you give me permission." I watched as he stepped outside his house. "I only wanted to pay my respects to Mabel."

"Well . . . get out of that dadblamed wreck of a truck, will you?"

"Sure." I reached for the door handle and it jammed. Damn. I'd have to do it the hard way. I curled my fingers around the roof and lifted myself out of the window, head first since I was wearing a blue jean sundress. Then I slithered my body out, careful not to flash too much leg in Everett's direction. Not that he'd probably notice. But, hey, I still had some shreds of modesty left.

When I finally cleared the window of my truck, I brushed off my sundress and grabbed the tiny package I'd picked up at Whiteside's on the way here. I waved it in Everett's direction.

"Okay, already," he grumbled. He wore the plaid shorts again, but obviously had gone for a more formal look by adding an undershirt. The front was stained with what appeared to be brown paint, but it could've been food or tobacco. I decided not to speculate further.

When I reached his porch, I halted and held out the little plastic bag.

He snatched it from me and peered inside.

"Does Mabel like toy mice?"

"She likes to kill real mice, but this one will do to train her to be more of a hunter."

Oh, goody. Everett can attack bunnies and maybe birds, while Mabel goes after the mice. They'd be a two-member attack team.

"Mr. Jacobs, I really didn't mean to harass you about Hillman's murder last time I was here—"

"Bullhockey. Snooping is part of your job." He lifted the catnip ball out of the bag and examined it.

"Uh . . . uh—" For once my motor mouth failed me.

"Go ahead, admit it. You think I'm an irascible old coot." He gave a short bark of laughter and I noticed his right incisor was missing. "It's true, I am. I don't like people and they don't like me."

I had to give him points for honesty.

"Everybody tries so hard to be nice all the time, when inside they're just seething with anger and resentment. I don't see any merit in holding back. It only makes you crazy. So, yes, I'm a mean old man and proud of it."

He scored a few more points.

"That's why I'm so attached to Mabel. Animals don't have no hidden motives. They either like you or hate you." He opened the screen door and tossed the catnip onto the porch. "She'll love that."

I heard a loud meow and the quick patter of claws against the tile floor.

"That's my Mabel. She moves faster than you can say 'jack rabbit'."

The word "rabbit" made me think of the BB gun again.

"Speaking of rabbits, I heard that the island has a problem with brown rabbits—"

"Damn right we do. They eat my hibiscus bushes right down to the stalk. Especially when there's no rain. There ain't no grass for them to nibble on, so they take to my plants." A sly grin peeped out from his bushy beard. "But I deal with 'em in my own way."

"And that is?"

He directed a penetrating stare at me. "That's for me to know."

Okay. Move on to another topic. "Looks like we might have a heck of a rainstorm brewing."

"Stop beating around the bush, missy. Go ahead and ask me."

I paused. "Did you murder Hillman?"

"Everybody thinks I did. Can't say I blame them. We argued constantly. We couldn't stand the sight of each other." He hooked his gnarled thumbs in the expansive waistband of his shorts. "If I didn't know better, *I'd* say I killed him."

"So you're saying you *didn't* murder him?"

"Thought about it lots of times . . . but I couldn't take another human life. Even if it was a low-down, nasty piece of work like Hillman. And that's exactly what I told Detective Billie."

I'm sure *that* was convincing. "He hasn't arrested you, so I guess that says something."

"I also have an alibi," he added.

"You do?"

"I just said I did."

"Okay. I was just affirming what you said." It was lame, I know. But nobody ever said I had the hang of questioning suspects yet.

He waved a hand in disgust. "I was on the mainland getting parts for my lawnmower, and I have witnesses who'll say they saw me there, too—around five P.M."

"You don't use the Island Hardware?" Keep him talking; he might trip himself up. Even if he went off the island, he had ample time to get back to the island and murder Hillman. *Weak alibi.*

"Them people? No way. Not since I found they were charging two dollars apiece more for a bag of nails. Told 'em so, too. We had a big blowup two years ago and I haven't been back since."

Now why didn't that surprise me? "What did Detective Billie say about your alibi?"

"Nothing. He don't use a lot of fancy words and waste my time." Everett gave me another pointed stare. "What about you, missy? You're a suspect 'cause you found the body. You got an alibi?"

"Not a specific one per say, but I had no motive to murder Hillman."

"Hah. Just knowing him was enough of a motive as far as I'm concerned."

"A few days ago I might've agreed with you but, since that time, I've found out a couple of things about Hillman that have made me see him in a new light. He wasn't a total jerk, by any means."

"Says you."

"Bradley Johnson seemed to like him."

"More's the fool."

"I thought I saw you with him this morning at the Starfish Lodge—"

"There you go snooping around again." His mouth pulled into a tight line.

"I wasn't snooping. I was meeting the writers' group there and just happen to see the two of you leaving," I hastened to defend myself. "It was sort of hard not to notice since you seemed to be having a disagreement with Bradley."

He cleared his throat and spit off to one side. "I stopped in to pick up a bagel—just minding my own business—and that fool comes up and tells me those rock crunchers up on the shell mounds—"

"The archaeologists?"

"Grave robbers if you ask me." He spit again. "They want to start digging a new site on the mounds—on the highest spot closest to my house. I told him no way any-how. I will not have all that commotion up there disturb-ing Mabel."

"And that's what you were arguing about?"

"Damn straight."

"What happened?"

"He saw my point of view." A flash of yellow teeth appeared. "And I'd better not see anybody up there or I'll . . ."

"Or you'll do what?" I prompted.

"Nothin'." He spit again and I stepped back. Either he was aiming for me or his vision was off, but I felt a sprinkle on my sandal. Yuck.

"I guess I'll be going." I didn't want to take a chance on where his next stream of spit was going to end up. "I hope Mabel feels tip-top soon. My own pet has been having some problems with local birds. They're all over Twin Palms and upset him to no end. Have you ever had that problem?"

"Nope. Mabel and I like birds. Especially the big vultures . . . they pick up roadkill and move on, cleaning up the roads and minding their own business."

"So you'd never harm a bird?"

"Why would I do that?" He began to clear his throat and I knew what was coming.

"Okay." I stepped back. "See ya."

Turning on my heel, I moved away just in time. His stream of spit barely missed my left foot.

I yanked on Rusty's driver's side door and, miraculously, it opened. I said a quick prayer to the saint of ancient, ramshackle cars and slid in behind the wheel. As I drove off, I peered in the rearview mirror. Everett was still standing there, watching me. I saw him crumple the brown bag containing the stuffed mouse and toss it on the ground. Oh, well, at least my catnip ball had been a hit.

No matter what he said, the jury was still out on whether he'd put the dead bird on my hood. And his alibi the night Hillman was murdered seemed shaky.

I headed back to Mango Bay, more than ready for the restful peace of the Twin Palms resort.

As soon as I drove up to my RV site, I scanned the picnic table. No more dead birds. Whew.

Humming in relief, I made for my Airstream, when I noticed a book on my top step. *Coral Island: Paradise Forgotten.* I leafed through it and a piece of paper fell out.

Dear Mallie,

The present is always tied to the past. You might find the answers you seek in these pages. At any rate, it makes better bedtime reading than bike path committee minutes.

Sam

Two notes in one day. I had to admit that our omnipotent handyman was on the ball.

Kong barked—reminding me that his little bladder was ready to burst.

"Okay, K.K., I'm here," I exclaimed as I swung the Airstream door open.

Kong came bounding out. I picked him up and buried my face in his soft apricot fur. "Sorry, buddy, I've been an all-around thoughtless airhead for leaving you so long." He licked my face in instant forgiveness. As I reveled in his complete and non-judgmental licks of love, I wondered why my family couldn't be like that? Accept me for who I am? I'm Mixed-up Mallie, and that's all there is to it.

All of a sudden, a thought rang with the clarity of a church bell inside of my mind. *Maybe it's time to grow up.* My eyes met Kong's. "What's happening to me? Is this what being involved in a murder investigation does to someone?" I inquired of him. He stopped licking my face.

A spurt of apprehension shot through me. Full-blown, four-alarm adulthood conjured up images of little white houses behind neat little picket fences in boring little towns. Serious. Nose-to-the-grindstone. Dull routines. *Oh, no. I'd become just like my parents.*

Mercifully, I was spared any further nightmarish speculation when the clouds finally opened up. Big, heavy drops fell on the back of my head and drizzled down my neck. I grabbed Kong's leash, took him for a quick walk, and lowered the awning of my Airstream. I'd been through tropical storms before, and this one promised to be in the words of Wanda Sue "a frogstrangler." My honeymooning neighbors had taken in their swimsuits and already closed their awning. No doubt they intended to ride out the storm in their own way.

Sighing, I battened down inside of my Airstream with only Kong and Sam's book for companionship.

Alone.

It *was* time to grow up.

The rain fell in torrential sheets most of the night, accompanied by wind gusts that roared through the trailer park like a rushing train. I was grateful for every one of the four thousand two hundred and twenty-five pounds of my Airstream as one blast of rain and wind passed through after another.

I tried reading the Coral Island history book for an hour or two, especially the part on the Caloosa Indians. I learned that they lived by hunting and fishing, but also had a complex social network all throughout Southwest Florida.

I was just getting to the part about ritual sacrifice when the power went out. I flipped the book shut, huddled under the covers with Kong, and tried to ignore the howling wind outside. Eventually, I must've dropped off to sleep because the next thing I knew it was morning. My Airstream intact, my body not yet sacrificed by the Caloosa, my dog snuggling in the crook of my arm. Hooray. I'd made it through the night, though still no power.

I peeped my head outside the Airstream. The sky, a gunmetal gray, looked threatening, and rain continued to fall in a gentle, steady rhythm. Evidence of last night's tumult appeared everywhere. Palm fronds lay scattered on the ground along with stray branches from nearby pine trees. Leaves, bits of garbage, and downed power lines gave the RV park a ragged, tattered look.

The behemoth next door survived, its generator humming.

I wondered if my honeymooning neighbors had even noticed that a storm had passed over.

"Howyadoing?" Wanda Sue said as she stopped at my site. A large garbage bag in one hand, a soft drink can in the other, she appeared to be a one-woman clean-up crew. Pop Pop Welch was no doubt occupied with his usual morning nap. Amazingly, her hair was still standing, not a hair out of place in its six-inch-high beehive.

"I made it through the storm." I stepped outside, checking to see if anyone else was around. I didn't particularly want anyone to see me in my knee-length

Mickey Mouse sleep shirt. I made a mental note that if I indeed intended to grow up, I probably needed to get rid of all my Mickey regalia—except the watch. I really loved the watch.

"We just made it through the first part of the storm," Wanda Sue said, picking up a crumpled paper plate. "The rest of the system is stalled a few miles out. We'll probably have more heavy rain for at least a couple of days."

"Will we have to evacuate?" For once, images of hooking up my Airstream behind Rusty didn't cause excitement to build inside of me. I wanted to stay and solve Hillman's murder.

"I don't think so—not yet. All around Mango Bay the power is out and there's standing water up to your wazoo." She pointed to her knees for emphasis. I thought the "wazoo" was located higher, but I could've been wrong.

"The roads are still passable, thank goodness," she continued. "We should be okay as long as the rain doesn't get too bad. But just to play it safe, be ready in case they announce an evacuation."

"What about the power? I really, really need a cup of coffee."

"Sorry . . . no go for a while." She shrugged. "All the RV's are going to have to rely on their generators for awhile."

Oh, boy. Needless to say, I didn't have one.

She strolled off, her industrial-size garbage bag trailing behind her. I was still momentarily entranced by her hair helmet, wondering how many cans of hair spray she went through each week.

I gave myself a mental shake and walked Kong. We didn't linger. I had things to do. People to see. A dark-haired detective in particular.

I took a quick, cold shower and donned my usual uniform of T-shirt and jeans, taking a few minutes to finger comb my curls. With the humidity so high and no air-conditioning, my hair resembled a cross between a bird's nest and brillo pad. Oh, well, it was the best I could do.

In half an hour I was on the road, maneuvering Rusty through the rain-soaked streets of Mango Bay. Water pooled in deep pockets, running with little currents across the road in low spots, and tree limbs lay scattered in lumpy piles. Luckily, my truck managed to lumber through the obstacles, and I was on Cypress Road, heading for the island center.

As I parked in front of the police station, only one car was in the parking lot—the black truck. Oh, goody. Just Detective Billie and me. He could berate me to his heart's content and no one would hear. I climbed out of Rusty. The driver's door was working again—why, I don't know. I'd just learned to accept my beloved truck's idiosyncrasies without question.

"Hello?" I called out as I stepped inside.

"Back here," Detective Billie said in a curt voice.

"How's it going?" I entered his office. He was on the phone barking orders to someone.

He nodded and motioned for me to take a seat. I decided to remain standing. If I didn't get too comfortable, I might get out of there sooner as opposed to later. That way, he couldn't browbeat me, and I could keep my heart from racing at the sight of his handsome face.

"There's no need to panic, Bob. We'll monitor the weather reports and decide our course of action in an orderly, careful manner. If, and I repeat, if we have to issue an evacuation order, we'll can do it through the emergency radio broadcast system," he was saying. "You'll have plenty of time to leave the island."

Salty Bob must've disagreed because Detective Billie frowned into the phone. "Look, I've got someone in the office I need to see. I'll call you back."

He hung up, muttering something under his breath.

"Don't tell me, Salty Bob is worried about his bike path easement flooding."

He nodded. "Every year it's the same thing. A little heavy rain and some wind, and people are ready to head for Tallahassee." He raked a hand through his dark hair and looked up at me. His eyes appeared tired, his face drawn with a five o'clock shadow that stretched to midnight. Darn. My heart already began to race. That ragged, edgy look was enough to make my engine hum.

"Uh . . . Did the storm keep you up last night?"

"That and the dozen calls from scared people in the flood zones."

"If my phone had been working, I might've been one of them."

He regarded me with a speculative gaze. "You don't strike me as the type to go all to pieces because of rain."

"Don't be too sure. This was my first tropical storm in my Airstream. The wind was enough to drive me whimpering under the covers with Kong—my dog," I informed him.

"He must be one heck of a big one to be named after a giant ape."

"Teacup poodle."

The phone rang again. He yanked it off the receiver and growled, "Billie, here. What is it? Bob, I said I'll call you back." He rolled his eyes and hung up. "He's not going to be satisfied till he's got everybody riled up."

"Is it going to get worse?" I was borderline riled myself, not looking forward to another night of fierce wind and rain.

"Doesn't look like it, but keep your radio on just in case."

Like I had a radio.

He took a long, deep drink of his coffee. The aroma wafted over to me and I immediately perked up. "Do you have any more of that stuff?" I gestured toward his large, white mug.

"In the reception area. Help yourself. Sorry I don't have any donuts."

"I thought the power was out on the island."

"We've got a generator."

Seems like everyone did—but me. I made a mental note to get a secondhand one as soon as I saved a few bucks. Ha.

Before you could say "cream or sugar," I dashed to the coffeepot and poured myself a steaming hot cup of my favorite adult stimulant. I could face anything after a couple of swigs—even Detective Billie's compelling aura.

"So what did you want to talk about?" I said as I reentered his office.

"You weren't really at the marina buying shrimp, were you?"

"Maybe not." I figured I could hem and haw for a while—at least until I got a second cup of coffee. "What do you think I was doing there?"

"I think you were trying to find Pete Cresswell so you could question him about Hillman's murder."

"Possibly." I downed half my styrofoam cup, ready to finish it off before I had to admit anything.

"No more coffee unless you answer my questions."

"You really know how to get a girl where it hurts, Billie."

"I've been known to withhold coffee for days at a time." Amusement touched his voice as he leaned back against the leather headrest of his chair. Did Detective Billie have a sense of humor? Was he actually teasing me, the woman who's been a thorn in his side since Hillman turned up dead?

"All right, you win. I admit I was there to question Pete." I took a seat opposite his desk. "I was talking to Nora; she said Pete had a grudge against Hillman, so I thought I'd have a friendly chat with him—for my article, of course."

"Of course." He wasn't buying it for a minute.

"Nora seemed worried that Pete might've killed Hillman. What do you think?" The best defense is a good offense—I'd heard that somewhere and decided it was worth a try.

"No comment."

Oh, well. "What did you want to talk to me about?"

"Maybe I wanted to see that red hair of yours again."

A tiny jolt moved through me. Was he flirting? Stiff-jawed, by-the-book, reserved Detective Billie? With his tousled hair and shadow of a beard that made me want to . . . whoa. Stop right there. He was the enemy—or at least off limits, at the very least.

"Okay, the real reason is I thought you'd like to know that I may be making an arrest shortly on the Hillman murder."

"Really? Who is it?" My excitement vied with my disappointment that I wasn't asked here so he could feast his eyes on my hair.

"I can't say."

"Everett Jacobs?"

"No comment."

"I knew it." My fists shot up in triumph.

"I'm not saying that he's the one. But since we're going to make an arrest, there's no point in continuing to question people. And, of course, you're off the hook as a suspect."

I lowered my arms. "Thanks for the vote of confidence."

"My pleasure."

"I expect a full statement from you for my next article—"

"You'll have it—after the arrest."

"I'll be waiting . . ." I rose to my feet. "Could I have another cup of coffee? The electricity is still out at the RV park and I didn't have my usual full pot this morning."

"Help yourself."

The phone rang again. He grabbed the receiver and motioned for me to close the office door on my way out. I complied, but was tempted to press my ear to the keyhole and see if I could catch any juicy tidbit, like when the arrest was going to be made. Unfortunately, the door had a modern brass knob with nary a keyhole in sight.

I contented myself with another cup of coffee. I had to admit Detective Billie made it just the way I liked It: strong to just-this-side of mud. Taking a deep swig, I stared at the closed door for a few moments. I had an absurd desire to say something else to him, but what?

Forget it. Not the right time—or place.

I turned away and made my way back out to Rusty.

The rain had stopped, but the sky was still overcast. A lull. That's all it was. The rain would start up again. I could smell it in the air.

I couldn't believe the investigation was almost over, and Everett would be arrested soon. I felt relieved, but vaguely uneasy. There were so many unanswered questions. I still hadn't talked to the boy that Hillman sponsored in Big Brothers/Big Sisters. And what about his financial state? Having writer's block for years must've put a dent in his savings, to say the least.

I climbed in my truck and fired up the engine.

Maybe those questions were unrelated to the murder. The untidy threads of a man's life that had unraveled and were left hanging with his unexpected death.

I pulled back onto Cypress Road and debated whether or not to stop at the Island Museum and talk to Bradley Johnson. If Everett were arrested in a day or two, knowing about the argument he had with Bradley the other night was a moot point. I should probably forget it.

I jerked the wheel to the right and turned into the museum parking lot. I couldn't resist. I'd come this far. Just because an arrest was going to be made, that didn't mean that I couldn't get the inside scoop.

A lone car stood in the semi-flooded parking lot. A low-slung Corvette, complete with T-tops and rear spoilers. Bradley drove that? For a few moments my vehicular psychoanalysis failed me. That kind of car was a testosterone machine, a blatant statement of "mine's-bigger-than-yours." A strange choice for a cultured type like Bradley. Even stranger to have that kind of car on a tropical island prone to flooding. Hmmm.

After I parked my truck, I entered the museum. It was a small, three-room building with giant glass cases that contained scenes of Caloosa life. Life-sized mannequins dressed and made-up to look like Caloosa peopled each case, along with to-scale models of rough huts. Realistic looking trees, flowers, and stuffed birds completed the settings.

"I didn't expect anyone to be out on a day like this," Bradley said as he came out from behind a desk. Wearing a splashy-print shirt and silk pants, he seemed a bit formally clothed for a museum curator. But I guess someone had to uphold fashion standards on Coral Island where most residents considered beach flip-flops "dress shoes."

"It's not so bad. Last night was the worst part by far."

"Your first tropical disturbance?" He pushed the large glasses back up his beaklike nose.

"No. But it's my first in a trailer."

"We'll probably have a little more rain—that's all." He smiled, but it didn't quite reach his eyes. "What can I do for you?"

"I wanted to look around a bit and . . . ask you about Everett Jacobs." Picking up a book, I flipped through it in feigned nonchalance. "I saw you two at the Starfish Lodge the other morning."

He grimaced. "We had a disagreement."

"Really?" I put the book down.

"I don't know what gets into Everett . . . he knows how important the archeological research is at the dig, but all he seems to be concerned about is that cat of his."

"Mabel is near and dear to his heart."

"But surely not more important than history."

"He said the research center wanted to expand the site."

Bradley shifted back and forth on his feet, as if suddenly nervous. "Well . . . yes. We want to do a separate dig on his side of the Mounds. It's too bad that Jack couldn't lay claim to the whole area—he totally supported the dig."

"I know. I heard that he donated a lot of the money for this museum, too."

"Yes, he was a great patron."

"Did he help with these displays?" I strolled around the glass cases. "They're so lifelike."

"No, I designed those—right down to the last detail."

All of a sudden, my eyes riveted on the stuffed birds. Had he done those, too? That would mean he'd have to have bird carcasses.

"I see you've noticed my birds." He had moved and positioned himself right behind me.

I eased a few steps away from him.

"A local taxidermist did them. I thought he did a terrific job."

"Yes, he did." I almost laughed at my own foolishness. Did I actually think Bradley could've killed a bird and stuffed it? What's more, maybe even put the egret on my picnic table? *Get real.* He doesn't even like to sweat.

"I'm reading about the Caloosa in a history book. They really lived quite a simple life, didn't they?"

"Yes, no money, no gold—just an idyllic life of fishing and living off the land. We could learn a lot from them."

"Sure." He droned on about the Caloosa, extolling their simple lifestyle and berating how we'd become too caught up in monetary gain. I felt like whipping out my checkbook and showing him the meager balance. I was already living close to subsistence level. The only difference between the Caloosa and me was that I didn't practice human sacrifice. "Look, I've got to swing by the *Observer* and make sure everything's okay . . . thanks for the tour."

"Anytime."

I ducked out of there before he could begin lecturing again. I'd gotten what I came for—he corroborated what Everett had said about their argument. Not that it probably mattered now.

As I drove off, I noticed the Corvette had a temporary license plate—the kind you get with a new car before your permanent plate comes through the mail. Not that I knew much about that. But my parents always bought a new car every three years, no matter what. So I'd seen the procedure many times.

It took me only about ten minutes to reach the strip mall at the island center where the *Observer* office was located. As I let myself in with my key, I realized Anita was already there. I could detect the unmistakable odor of her Camels.

"Hey, kiddo. You keeping high and dry?" she exclaimed from inside her cubicle.

"Sort of." I halted at the threshold, deciding to limit my exposure to the life-threatening miasma of her second-hand smoke. "I came by to check on the office. Everything looks okay."

"Yeah, this place is pretty sturdy." She tapped her feet on the shabby linoleum floor. A hollow, ringing sound echoed through the office. "I've got an advance copy of this week's paper. Your story on Hillman looks . . . not bad."

I smiled. High praise, indeed. "I heard on the Q.T. that Detective Billie would be making an arrest soon."

Anita pursed her wrinkled mouth. "He told you?"

"Yeah."

"Now that's interesting. I wouldn't have thought he'd be close to an arrest yet." She propped her feet up on the desk and folded her arms behind her head. "He must've found out that Pete's alibi didn't hold up—"

"Pete? I thought he was going to arrest Everett Jacobs," I protested.

"That old fool? Not in this lifetime."

"But—"

"Pffft. Nick Billie isn't stupid enough to take what

that old man says seriously, and you shouldn't either, kiddo."

I glared at her. "How did you know about Pete?"

"Everybody's heard about the affair that Nora had with Hillman. It just makes sense that he had the greatest motive—jealousy."

"But what about your mantra, 'follow the money'—" A loud clap of thunder interrupted me.

"I might've been wrong." She dropped her arms and sat up straight. "Right now, you'd better go on back to the Twin Palms and ride out the rest of this storm." Anita waved me out.

I wasn't convinced about Pete's guilt, but I didn't need to be told twice to go home. I knew Kong would be nervous as heck with more stormy weather ahead.

First, I drove to Whiteside's at Mango Bay and purchased four gallons of water, bread, toilet paper, dog food, and the latest copy of *People* magazine. I figured if I got bored with the history book, I could read about how anorexia was taking over Hollywood's starlets.

When I parked to the side of my Airstream, I noticed most of the debris left by the storm had been cleared away. Go, Pop Pop. My site looked neat and tidy—ready for the next go around with the elements. And I was, too.

I exited Rusty, bags in hand, when all of a sudden, an odd shivery feeling snaked through me. Just like when I found the dead egret on my picnic table. Oh, no. Not again.

I halted. My gaze slowly panned around the RV site. Nothing seemed amiss, nothing unusual.

I gasped as my eyes came to rest on the front of my Airstream.

Someone had slashed my two front tires.

"I don't believe this. A moron came into the park and did this in broad daylight," I said aloud. I ran my hand over one of the tires. Yep, it had been slashed all right. I could feel the deep groves the blade had carved into the rubber. Tears stung at the back of my eyes as I banged my head against the trailer in frustration.

Just then, a battered white truck pulled up. I thought it impossible to drive a vehicle more dingy than Rusty, but this one had even more dents and scratches.

Nora stuck her head out the window. "Mallie, you've got to help me. They're going to arrest Pete—"

"Oh, no!" Damn. Anita had nailed it.

"He's hiding out on Little Coral Island and says he won't let them take him in." Eyes wild, hair uncombed, she clutched the steering wheel with shaky hands.

"I don't know what I can do—"

"Please, you're the only person I've been able to talk to who believes that I still love him. Help me to get him turn himself in."

"I . . . uh . . . all right." I opened the Airstream door, threw in the grocery bags, and checked to see if Kong was okay. He wagged his tail in usual chipper fashion. I locked everything up carefully.

"Mallie, hurry." Nora began crying.

I opened the driver's side door of Nora's truck. Interestingly, it squeaked just like mine. "Scoot over. You're in no shape to drive."

She complied.

"Is Pete armed?" I asked as I took the wheel.

"No . . . yes. I don't know," she babbled. "He might have a gun."

Great. Just great. An armed ex-con. What was I getting myself into? I paused.

Nora sobbed harder. "Please!"

I rammed the truck into gear and hit the gas pedal.

Chapter Ten

As I steered Nora's truck onto Cypress Road, I reached up to adjust the rearview mirror. It fell off in my hand. I set it on the dashboard and realized I'd have to make do with the side mirror. I glanced out the window. Also gone.

Okay, so much for the need to see what's behind us.

Luckily, traffic was nonexistent and, luckier still, some of the tree branches had been shoved to the side of the road.

"Nora, try to calm down and tell me what happened." I pressed the pedal down to the floor, and the speed increased only about five miles per hour. This was going to be a long drive.

She wiped the tears away with the back of her hand and blew her nose in a crumpled tissue. "I felt sort of . . . I don't know, hopeful after we talked yesterday. So I tracked Pete down at a friend's house—to tell him that I still love him. When I got there, Detective Billie pulled up behind me, said he wanted to see Pete. I freaked out and started screaming. Pete must've heard and lit out the back door." She choked and swallowed a sob. "He yelled out that he'd never go back to jail."

"What did Detective Billie do?"

"I expected him to jump in his car and take off after him, but he just watched Pete leave. Said he didn't want to panic Pete into doing something stupid."

"Good for him." Maybe he wasn't totally a by-the-book kinda of cop.

"No one has seen Pete since, but I think I know where he might be. His grandpa used to run a still in the mangroves out on Little Coral Island, and there's a small shack there. Not too many people know about it because it's hard to find and you can only get to it by way of a one-lane, dirt track road."

"The road must be like mush. Can we get through with all the rain we had yesterday?"

"I . . . I think so." She bit her lip.

"It might've dried out today. We can only hope that it won't start raining again." As if on cue, raindrops splattered against the windshield. Oh, no. I rammed the pedal down again, trying to get every ounce of power out of the truck. The speedometer stayed at forty-five and stubbornly refused to move.

"Tell me where to turn," I said.

"Make a left turn on Bayview—that'll take you past a saw palmetto strand. Most people think the road ends there, but it doesn't. It circles around to an itty-bitty spit of land that connects to Little Coral Island."

"Okay, I'm game." I continued down Cypress Road for another couple of miles, managing to nudge the truck's speed up to almost fifty. I smelled a burning odor, but refused to let up. The rain was coming harder, faster, and the truck's windshield wipers didn't work much better than Rusty's.

"Here's the turn," Nora exclaimed.

I yanked the wheel to the left and the back tires skidded, causing the flatbed part of the truck to fishtail. I compensated by jerking the wheel to the left and, somehow, we held the road.

"Dang, that's some fancy driving," Nora commented.

"I spent a couple of months operating the Pirates of the Caribbean ride at Disney World." What that had to do with driving a car, I don't know, but it seemed relevant.

"Pete and I honeymooned there." She sighed. "It was so romantic."

I had no response to that. I was working hard to keep the truck on the shell road and see through the rain so we wouldn't end up ditched.

"Slow down and steer around to the left."

I peered through the windshield and spied the saw palmetto.

"Okay, now veer down that dirt track," she said.

"Where?" I couldn't even see anything that resembled a raccoon track, must less a road.

"Over there." She pointed at a break in the strand and I steered the truck in that direction.

The poor truck lurched and bumped its way along the rough road while the rain pelted down on us. I eased up some more on the gas pedal, but we were still going forty-five. I hit the brakes, but nothing happened.

"Nora, I can't slow down."

"Oh, it's that dorky gas pedal. It sticks. Just give it a couple of stomps and it'll behave."

Knowing I couldn't go much faster and keep control of the truck, I pumped the gas pedal. Finally, the speedometer inched back down.

I still couldn't see much of a road, so I just followed along the trimmed area. It seemed almost like a tunnel with pine trees and melaleuca arching around us from either side.

We emerged into a clearing and lumbered over a sand and shell track that took us onto Little Coral Island. The wheels stuck a few times, but I refused to stop now we were so close.

"Does anyone live on Little Coral Island?" I asked.

"Not now. But at one time, Pete's grandpa homesteaded around here with his partner, Pappy. I think Pappy ran the still and Grandpa tried his luck with a citrus grove."

"Nice combo."

"They made a living till Grandpa died. Pappy

stayed—then he died. The last couple years, you could see him if you went by in your boat, half naked, holding a jug and waving people on in."

"What is it with Coral Island men and clothes? Do they all go around bare-chested or what?"

"I don't think so. Pappy was the only one I know who did it regularly. And gosh, he was near to ninety before he expired—and looking like a scrawny chicken, if you ask me."

Too much information. I thought seeing Hillman and Everett bare-chested was traumatic. Pappy must've had them beat to all getout.

"We should be there in—" She drew in a sharp breath. "Oh, no."

I followed her glance. Detective Billie's truck was parked in front of the shack and he stood next to it, soaked from head to toe in the rain.

Cautiously, I applied pressure to the brakes, and miraculously, the truck slowed down. *Small miracles.*

We climbed out and went to join Detective Billie. The rain immediately plastered our clothes to our bodies. When he saw us, his mouth tightened into a straight line. "What are you doing here?" he ground out between clenched teeth.

"We thought we'd work on our suntans," I quipped.

"Very funny. Now get out of here so I can do my job."

"Are you going to arrest Pete?" Nora blurted out.

"I have to," he said, wiping the rain from his face.

"His fishing knife was found near Hillman's house. It's unmistakable—carved handle with Pete's initials—and it fits the size of Hillman's chest wound."

"But that doesn't mean he killed him." She clutched at Detective Billie's shirt. "He didn't, I know it. Please don't arrest him. He said he couldn't go back to jail. *Please.* He's got an alibi. He was out fishing when Jack was killed." Her voice reached a high pitch, close to a wail.

Something flickered behind Detective Billie's eyes. Sympathy? Regret? I couldn't make it out because my vision was blurry from the rain.

"Nora, his alibi said Pete asked him to lie about where he was the night Hillman was murdered. I have to take him in." He gently removed her hands from his shirt.

"I'm not coming out," Pete shouted from inside the shack.

"Yes you are, Pete," Detective Billie shouted back. "Come on and make it easy. The other way makes you look more guilty."

"How do know he did it?" I finally piped up. "There are other suspects—"

"I'm not asking for your opinions, Mallie. This isn't the time or place for a debate. Either shut-up or leave." His tone was firm, final.

But I plunged on recklessly. "Isn't it possible that someone stole Pete's knife, knowing how much he disliked Hillman because of Nora's affair—"

"It wasn't really an affair," she cut in. "We were just friends."

"Right. Anyway, that person could be setting Pete up."

That muscle began working in Detective Billie's jaw again. "You've been watching too much TV."

"But it's possible," I persisted.

"Theoretically, yes."

"Then tell Pete that . . . let him know that this isn't the end of the line for him." Our eyes met in the rain. His black as night—that deep, dark obsidian that seemed to lead to places I couldn't even fathom.

"Please, Nick, give him a chance," Nora pleaded.

He paused, still staring down at me. "All right." Turning toward the shack, he cupped his hands around his mouth and shouted, "Pete, I promise that you'll have a fair shake. You're innocent until proven guilty. Trust me."

"No way."

"Let Nora talk to him," I suggested.

"Oh, jeez—okay." He gestured for her to move toward the shack.

"Pete, this is Nora. Please come with us. I know you didn't do it. That's what I came to tell you last night—"

"Forget it," he yelled back.

"Go on," I encouraged her.

"It's true. There was nothing between Jack Hillman and me when you were in jail. Nothing. You've got to believe me. I've tried to tell you so many times."

Pete was silent.

"Keep it up," I said.

"I'll stand by you no matter what happens. You're my husband."

"Tell him that you love him," I prompted.

Detective Billie groaned.

"Pete, honey, I love you. I love you so much. Please come out so we have a chance."

Silence.

"Tell him—"

"That's enough," Detective Billie interjected as he reached for his gun. "He's not coming out."

The door to the shack slowly opened and a thin, brown-haired man wearing jeans and a black T-shirt appeared in the doorway.

"Pete," Nora exclaimed as she broke into a run toward the shack. She threw herself in his arms and sobbed against his chest.

"It's okay, baby. It'll all be okay," I could hear him saying to her.

The rain kept falling, and Detective Billie and I stood still as if we'd been turned to stone. Finally, he cleared his throat and holstered his gun. "You're damn lucky things turned out like this or I'd be arresting you for obstruction of justice."

"I didn't obstruct anything."

"I ordered you to leave and you refused," he answered swiftly.

"I don't take orders well."

"You will when it comes to the safety—"

"Oh, give it up, will you? You just can't accept help when someone offers it," I retorted.

"If I needed help, I'd hire a deputy."

"Fat chance you'd get anyone—"

"Hey you two, time out," Nora said as she and Pete approached. "The important thing is it all came out okay."

"Do you have to cuff me?" Pete held his hands out.

"No, just get in my truck."

A slight, sheepish smile touched Pete's mouth and he shoved his hands in his jeans pockets. "Thanks, Nick. I appreciate it. I was stupid, I know . . ."

"And you two," he leveled a frown at Nora and me, "follow me back to the police station."

I started to open my mouth and he held up a weary hand. "Could you do this one thing without arguing for a change?"

"All right." I had to admit, I was a bit tired of standing in the rain. I'd sort of lost feeling in my feet about fifteen minutes ago, and I had to clench my teeth to keep them from chattering.

"Will wonders never cease?" he muttered, half to himself. Nora and I stumble-bummed back to her truck and I cranked the ignition. The battery was dead. I closed my eyes and lowered my head against the steering wheel. What next?

After wasting another fifteen minutes in the pouring rain while Detective Billie and Pete tried to jump Nora's battery, we gave up. I grabbed my canvas bag, and we climbed into the sleek, black truck owned by our fearless chief deputy—Nora and Pete in the backseat, Detective Billie and I in the front seat.

No one spoke on the long drive back to the police station. Nora sniffed, Pete coughed, and I sneezed. Detective Billie sat behind the wheel, his face set in grim lines.

When we arrived, our motley, rain-sodden group trooped inside. Detective Billie found some towels and we dried off as best we could.

"Whew," Nora exclaimed, rubbing the terry cloth up and down her arms with vigorous strokes. Her hair was plastered to the side of her face in long, limp strands, the roots appearing even darker and the blond sections even lighter. "I ain't never seen so much rain since that hurricane skirted the island back in ninety-seven."

"I remember," Pete echoed, drying off his face. "My boat ended up on shore after the tides went out."

"And you had to get some of the guys to lift it onto the trailer so you could move it back to the water," Nora said, laughing. "I'll never forget the sight of those men struggling to lift a twenty-two-foot with twin outboard engines."

"It would've helped if you'd removed the engines," Detective Billie pointed out as he rubbed his dark hair with the towel. "I told you—"

"They'd had too many beers in them by that time." Nora snapped her towel against Pete's jean-clad leg.

"We needed fortification." Pete grabbed the towel from her and smiled.

"Yeah, and it worked like a charm." Detective Billie rolled his eyes.

"Didn't mean to drop the boat," Pete mumbled.

"Uh-huh." Nora elbowed him in the ribs. They all chuckled.

I blinked the last of the water away from my eyes, concerned that I had stumbled out of the rain and into an alternative reality. "I'm sure this trip down memory lane is nice, but we just arrested Pete. And I hardly think this is the time for jokes. Shouldn't we call an attorney for him or something?"

The three of them turned to me and the laughter ceased.

"Just trying to lighten the moment," Nora offered with a sheepish smile. "And it ain't like we haven't been through this before the last time Pete was sent up."

"But that wasn't murder," I continued.

"She's right," Detective Billie cut in, his features resuming their normal granite-like firmness. "Pete, I'm going to have to lock you up."

He took in a breath and exhaled in a long, drawn-out sigh. "I know."

"Can I sit back there with him?" Nora asked. It might've been my imagination or that alternative reality thing again, but her face had softened in the last few hours. She looked about ten years younger. "We've got some things to talk over."

"Sure." Detective Billie led them through a doorway in the back, where the cells were located. Or, rather, cell. I could only make out one.

I took the opportunity to finish drying off, giving my hair a few quick fluffs with the towel.

When Detective Billie returned, I pounced. "I still can't believe that you arrested him. You're . . . friends."

"It's my job." He gathered up the damp towels. "Weren't you reminding me a few minutes ago that I was taking this whole thing too lightly? Well, I'm not. I don't like it anymore than you do. But I have to uphold the law." He threw the towels on the sofa in a wet, soggy heap. "Pete's knife was found with blood on it, he has no alibi, and he hated Hillman. That makes him the prime suspect and he'll stay in jail until the blood analysis comes back. If it matches with Hillman's, then . . ." His voice trailed off as he looked down, but we both knew the unspoken words.

"What about Everett? Or the writers at the Institute? They're all suspects. And any of them could've been the one who's been threatening me."

His face jerked up. "What are you talking about?"

Oops. "Well . . . I wasn't going to tell you because I knew you'd make a big deal about it and, you know, I've been asking a lot of questions around the island. Probably making people uncomfortable and everything, so it's possible—"

"Will you get to the point?" he demanded.

"I was getting there." It was nice to know the rain

hadn't damaged the engine on my motor mouth. "Friday night, someone put a dead bird on the picnic table outside my Airstream. Then a few hours ago, I went back to the RV resort and found my tires slashed. The front ones. So you see, that couldn't have been Pete. He was out on Little Coral Island when my tires were cut."

"And exactly when were you going to tell me about all of this?"

"When I felt you needed to know." I turned my chin up on a stubborn angle. "Nothing happened, no one was injured. Why that bird could've had a stroke or something and fallen out of the sky onto my picnic table for all I know."

"Oh, yeah, that's a real possibility." Sarcasm dripped from his tongue. "Even if I believed that, which I don't, the tires are another matter."

"That's my point. Pete couldn't have done it."

"It doesn't mean he didn't murder Hillman."

I gritted my teeth. He had me there.

"Stay out of this investigation. I've already made the arrest, and we'll let the attorneys take it from here." He drilled a stare into me. "You breeze onto the island a few weeks ago, and now suddenly you think you're some kind of Ms. Fix-it crack reporter, solving everyone's problems. It doesn't work that way. You don't understand what's happening, and you're not going to do anything but hurt Pete and Nora by interfering."

"Or maybe save them."

His mouth tightened, but he didn't respond.

"Just give me a day or two—"

"If you need a ride back to the Twin Palms, I'd be happy to oblige; otherwise, your part in this drama is over."

"I can find my own way back." I slammed out of the office in what I hoped appeared to be a grand exit. But my canvas bag caught in the door and I couldn't go far. Detective Billie opened the door again and released me. "Thanks," I managed to get out before I left and plunged into the rain once more. I'd be damned if I'd ride with him after he basically told me I was nothing but an outsider on the island. That wasn't true. I felt a kinship with this place and the people who lived here. Heck, I'd just put myself out for the first time in my life for someone other than myself. That should count for something.

Even more irritating, his behavior showed me for once and all that this attraction thing was one sided. On the wrong side.

I hunched my shoulders, trying to protect my bag from the rain. Maybe I didn't understand all the island nuances but, in spite of all the craziness, this was beginning to feel like home.

I looked up and the rain pelted my face. Oh, goody. I finally found a place to call home and I'd probably get flooded out before the day was over.

I kept walking.

Chapter Eleven

Fortunately, Wanda Sue came driving by in her vintage convertible in less than half an hour and picked me up.

As we made our way back to Mango Bay, she clucked her tongue when I told her about my tires being slashed.

"First the murder, then the dead bird, and now the tires. What's the island coming to?" she asked. "I'm going to have Pop Pop patrol twice a night."

That'll be a big help. I didn't respond, just clenched my jaw to keep my teeth from chattering.

When we pulled up in front of my Airstream, I thanked her and trudged out of her car. My shining silver abode never looked so good, in spite of the flat tires. After I walked Kong, I headed for the shower. As I leaned against the tile and let the hot, steaming water warm me, I began to cry. It all seemed too much. The murder. The dead bird. The tires. Pete's arrest. Being a part of a community was taxing, to say the least.

I crawled into bed, pulled the covers over my head and dropped into a deep slumber. For almost ten hours.

The next morning, I woke up to a watery dawn. The sun tried to peep out as though it were a flickering flashlight in desperate need of new batteries.

I was roughly in the same state. And I didn't know where I could recharge.

A slobbery tongue licked the rim of my ear, and I laughed softly. Of course, it wasn't a human and not exactly an energy jolt, but it would do just fine. I slipped an arm around Kong and hugged him tightly.

I flipped back the covers and padded into the kitchen. Empty fridge. Empty cupboards—aside from the bread and water. But at least I had power again. That meant the rest of the island probably did, too. *Hooray*!

What I needed was a pot of coffee and donuts . . . lots of donuts.

Fueled by hunger, I quickly dressed in a white cotton tank top and a fresh pair of jeans, giving my curls the merest flick with the brush.

"Check back with you, Kong." I blew him a kiss and was out the door.

Half an hour later, I strolled into the *Observer* office, coffee and half-eaten donut in hand. Okay, so it wasn't my first.

"Big doings yesterday," Sandy remarked. "I heard

Pete was arrested and you were the one that got him to give himself up."

I shook my head as I seated myself at the computer. "It was Nora who persuaded him. She's the one that deserves all the credit."

"That's not what the Jordan sisters said." She smiled and snapped the rubber band on her wrist.

"What's that for?"

"A little cognitive diet therapy. Every time I have a food craving, I snap the band." She gave a little demonstration. "Eventually, I'll come to associate food with pain and I won't want to eat anymore."

I couldn't argue with that logic.

"Hey, kiddo. When are you going to get started on the story of Pete's arrest?" Anita stood in the doorway to her little cubicle, bony arms folded across her chest.

Leave it to Anita to understand that I might need some down time to let yesterday's events sink in. "He was arrested, but I don't think he did it."

"Not your problem," she continued.

"It is when I was part of the arrest."

Her thin lips grew even thinner. "Your job is to report the news, not make it. Pete was arrested. He's the prime suspect in Hillman's murder. That's your story."

"I understand." Do the story, or I'm fired. Anita always reduced things to the simplest level. "But first I want to do a little digging this morning on a couple of loose ends. I don't need to have the article done for a few days, and I want to make sure that I've followed up on all the leads on Hillman—"

"Suit yourself, but I'll need time to edit your copy." She ambled back into her cubicle. "I'll be working on a story about the tropical storm damage, so unless someone charges in here with a gun, don't disturb me."

I had a sudden, childish urge to stick my tongue out at her, but with my newfound sense of adult responsibility, I figured that was out. I satisfied my urge by giving her a surreptitious and extremely rude hand gesture under the desk.

"Sandy, can I use your phone? I need to make a call to Miami."

"Sure. It's time for my morning meditation." She pulled out the iPod, clamped it over her head, and began doing that "ommmmmm" sound. I never could figure out what was relaxing about sounding like the signal on an emergency broadcast band, but who was I to argue with success? She wasn't wearing any visible price tags this morning, so something was working.

I dialed the Miami number of Hillman's "Little Brother" and a woman answered.

"Could I speak to Todd Griffith?" I asked in my most polite tone.

"Just a minute." She covered the lower half of the phone, but I could still hear her scream out his name.

"I got it," a young man's voice came onto the line and the woman hung up.

"Hi, my name is Mallie Monroe and I work for the

Coral Island Observer. I'd like to ask you a couple of questions about Jack Hillman, if you don't mind."

A pause. "I guess I don't."

"I can tell by your tone that you must've heard about what happened to him."

"Yeah, it was in the *Herald*. I was sorry 'cause, you know, he was like a really good guy."

"So I've heard." At least from you, and that makes a majority of one. "How did you meet him?"

"He was my Big Brother when I was in middle school. I'd just lost my dad, and my mom was working full-time running a daycare. I was pretty mad at the world . . . and doing stuff that I shouldn't have been doing. Anyways, Jack helped me, got me interested in sports, made me want to make something of myself."

I jotted all of this down in my official reporter's notepad.

"He even helped my mom go back to school so she could become a teacher. She got a job here in Miami and we moved in with my grandmother about three years ago."

"Did you keep in contact with Mr. Hillman?"

"Oh, yeah. He helped me with my college applications this year. I'm a freshman starting this fall." A tinge of pride touched his voice. "Jack even set up a trust fund for me to help with the tuition, but I got a Bright Future's Scholarship. Full ride and a stipend. I was going to tell him last week, but I was . . . too late."

"I'm sure he would've been proud of you, Todd."

And I meant it. "Did Mr. Hillman ever say that he was having financial problems?"

"No. Leastways, I don't think so. I know he was having trouble writing, but he said he'd found a 'money tree'—that's how he put it. And that I shouldn't worry about affording college."

"Did he say what that 'money tree' was?"

"'Fraid not."

"Okay. Thanks, Todd, you've been a great help."

"I hope they catch his killer . . . he's got to be a real sicko."

"Yeah, I agree." I hung up and spent a few minutes glancing over my notes. Hillman had found another way of making money. That was the key. "Follow the money," Anita had said, and she was right. Wherever that cash was coming from—that's where I'd find his murderer. And it sure wasn't Pete.

The door swung open and my great aunt stepped in with Sam at her side. "How are you doing this morning, Mallie?" she inquired. "I don't want you to think we're checking up on you, but that's exactly what we're doing. Heard you had quite a time of it yesterday."

"The Jordan sisters?"

"Who else?" She smiled. "They've staked out the picnic aisle at the Island Hardware, telling everybody who cares to listen about your part in the arrest yesterday."

"My part was small."

"Not the way they tell it."

I looked from her to Sam. He'd changed his "enigma" T-shirt for a wrinkled, white one that had some kind of Chinese inscription painted across the front in bold black. Still wearing the gold stud, he'd freshly trimmed his remaining hair to a close crop. Not quite the scruffy professor—merely tousled.

"Are you okay?" He seemed to be studying me as though I were a specimen under glass.

"I was pretty wiped out last night, but I'm all right to-day." I glanced over at Sandy. Eyes closed, humming away, she was in her own world. Good. I leaned in closer to Sam and Aunt Lily. "But I'm not sure Detective Billie arrested the right person. I don't know. It seems off to me."

"Best to let the police handle it." Aunt Lily patted my hand. "Nick Billie knows what he's doing."

"What do you think, Sam?" I asked.

"Your aunt is a wise woman. Let events take their natural course. This is a police matter."

"I guess so." Doubts still assailed me, but were they based in reality or the misguided hope that Pete wasn't a murderer? "Maybe I just want to believe that Nora has a future with her husband that doesn't include more jail time—or worse."

"Mallie, remember when you were just a kid and you kept trying to catch bees?" Aunt Lily's voice was quiet.

"Yeah, I wouldn't give up."

"Until you got stung. Then you stopped."

"I'll say." I shuddered in remembrance. "My hand blew up like a baseball mitt."

"Exactly. This is the same thing." Aunt Lily wagged a wrinkled finger in my direction. "I don't want to see you get stung."

"I get it." And I didn't like it. Going off half cocked without any backup plan was my specialty. But I'd changed. At least I thought about what I was doing before I did it. That was a start.

"Let it be for a couple of days and see what happens," she said.

"Okay," I grudgingly gave in.

"Come over for dinner tonight and we'll talk. You can fill us in on what happened yesterday. I'm sure the Jordan sisters left something out." She bent over my desk to plant a kiss on top of my head. "It's that red hair, Carrot. It's a curse."

"Takes one to know one."

She laughed. "We'll see you later."

"Hey, Sam, I forgot to thank you for the history book. I'm not sure how it relates to the murder, but I've learned a lot about the Caloosa Indians."

He inclined his head slightly. "Knowing the past will give you insights to the present. It works for me every time."

Aunt Lily raised her eyes to the ceiling and groaned. "Don't encourage her, Sam."

"Sam has helped me. He's the one who put me onto Nora in the first place."

He stared at me blankly.

"The note—you left it on my truck?" I prompted. "It said to talk to Nora at the Seafood Shanty."

"I never put a note on your truck."

"But you stopped by the Lodge the other morning and said you had information for me—"

"I wanted you to get the Caloosa history book—then I went ahead and checked it out of the library and left it at your trailer."

My eyes met his. *Whoa*. Someone had wanted me to talk to Nora and throw me off track—implicate Pete. And that someone could be Hillman's murderer. I'd bet my last donut on it. Oh, no. I forgot. I'd already eaten it.

I said nothing but felt in my bones that I was right. The murderer was still loose on the island.

After I promised Aunt Lily to have dinner with her and Sam the next day, I reluctantly turned my attention to the story about Pete's arrest. It was the last thing I wanted to do when my mind was begging to go over the list of possible suspects who could've put that note on my truck: Everett? Chrissy? George? Burt and Betty? Scooby-Doo? My head ached.

And much as I didn't want to write the article, I knew Anita would come breathing down my neck soon if I didn't. And her smoke-filled breath was not a smell to be taken lightly.

I pounded out a couple of paragraphs, watched Sandy snap her rubber band a dozen or so times, and downed another coffee before I packed it in for the afternoon. "I'm going back to the Twin Palms for a break," I informed Sandy. She waved me out with yet another snap of the rubber band. Her wrist was turning red, the skin beginning to swell. She'd be lucky ever to want to eat again after her bout with cognitive diet therapy.

As I drove Rusty toward Mango Bay, I opened my window and enjoyed the cool breeze coming in off the Gulf. The rain had finally stopped. The sun hadn't fully appeared from behind the clouds yet, but it was on the verge. Thin shoots of light already managed to eek out little paths of warmth, so it was only a matter of time before we'd receive a full blast of sunshine again. And I'd have to slather on the sunblock again.

I checked my peeling nose in the rearview mirror. Only the barest pink. Goody. One more cloudy day and I'd have a semi-normal nose again.

When I reached my RV site, I glanced at the flat tires. I'd need to order two new ones and have Pop Pop put them on—if his arthritic hands could handle the jack.

My honeymooning neighbors had opened their awning again. They were still alive.

I put the leash on Kong, grabbed the Coral Island

history book, and made for the beach. He immediately balked. "Nope, it's time to get over this beach thing, K.K. This is our home now and you've got to stop being scared of the water."

I tried gently to tug him in the direction of the waves. No go. Then, I yanked a bit harder. He dug in with surprising strength for a little hair mop. "All right. That's enough." I scooped him up in my arms and walked toward the small beach. "We're going to stay here until you face your fears."

I slipped the leash around my wrist and plopped down in the sand. Kong whined, then tucked his head under my knee. "Well, that's a start." I set the book on my legs and idly flipped the pages, skimming the section about the Caloosa Indians. Nothing new. I started to move on to the pirate days when something caught my eye. A picture of a Caloosa man. Tall and thin with a weathered face and long, dark hair. Not much clothing. Wearing gold beads around his neck and carrying a knife with a decorated gold hilt. Gold. He was wearing gold.

Bradley had been mistaken. The Caloosa *did* trade in gold. There could actually be valuable artifacts in the dig on the Mounds. Wouldn't he have known that? Or wasn't he as smart as he pretended?

I snapped the book shut and pulled Kong out from under my leg. Maybe that's why Hillman wanted sole ownership of the mound behind his house. He was doing a little digging of his own. Was it possible he'd found the jackpot? Were the Caloosa artifacts his "money tree"?

"Okay, Kong, you're off the hook for now." I jumped to my feet and brushed the sand off my jeans. "I've got to make a couple of calls." I hustled Kong back to the Airstream, almost running in my eagerness to question Bradley.

I reached for the phone as soon as I made it inside, and rang the historical museum. "Come on. Come on," I chanted.

"Hello, you've reached the Coral Island Historical Museum. I'm Bradley Johnson, curator. Please leave a message at the tone, and I'll return your call as soon as humanly possible. Have a great day."

I gritted my teeth. "Bradley, this is Mallie Monroe. I need to talk to you about something. Call me, please." I left my number and hung up.

Just then the phone rang.

"Hello?"

"Mallie, this is Chrissy. How-ya-doing?"

"Pretty good."

"Just thought you might like to join us at the Starfish for a drink. Now that this Pete guy has been arrested, some of our group is leaving tomorrow. This is sort of our farewell get together."

I hesitated. But then I realized Chrissy might know something about the artifacts, and this might be my last chance to talk to her. "Sure, I'll be right over."

"Great. George is here already here."

I hung up, gave Kong a quick hug, and left. I was getting close.

A few minutes later, I was on Cypress Road heading for the Starfish Lodge. On a whim, I decided to swing by the Henderson Research Center at the Mounds—just on the chance that Bradley might be there. As I came around the road in front of Hillman's house, I didn't see Bradley's car, but I did spy an old model Cadillac with New Mexico license plates in Hillman's driveway. Burt and Betty. What were they doing here?

I pulled in behind their car and quietly slid out of my truck. Even though I knew it was illegal, I ducked under the yellow police tape and made for the house. Drawing closer, I tiptoed across the screened front porch. I heard voices within. Definitely Burt and Betty. There were inside the house. Why?

I eased the screen door open and stepped onto the porch. Then I crept around the living room toward the hallway. Burt and Betty were in the office—the place where Hillman had been murdered.

"We've finally got the proof we need," Burt was saying.

"Thank goodness. After two years. We can show the world what Hillman did to us," Betty said.

Some shuffling of papers and books.

"I'm sorry he was killed, but what he did to us was wrong, and it has to come out. Now they've caught his killer, we can go public with the truth," Burt added.

"Maybe we should wait." Betty's tone was tentative, worried.

Burt gave an exclamation of impatience. "But we've waited so long. It isn't fair."

What the heck were they talking about? I felt fairly certain at this point that they weren't the killers, so I strode down the hallway and burst in on them. "What are you doing in here?"

Betty screamed and dropped the papers in her hands. Burt grunted and clutched his chest. His knees buckled and he slid to the floor.

"Oh, no." Betty rushed to his side. "Now look what you've done. You should know better that to sneak up on us like that. Burt has angina." She pressed her hands to the side of his florid face.

I shifted from one foot to the other, not sure if I should call the police or the paramedics.

She glared at me. "If you've killed him, I'll never forgive you."

Chapter Twelve

I'll call 911," I finally said.

"No," Burt and Betty exclaimed simultaneously. "We can't be caught here. We crossed the yellow tape."

"But Burt could be having a heart attack." I looked him over. His face, always florid, had heated up to a color close to the shade of my hair.

"Nope, I'm okay," he wheezed. "Just get me into a chair and I'll catch my breath."

"Are you sure?" I looked from him to Betty and back again. They both nodded. "All right." I took one of his arms and Betty the other, and we somehow managed to hoist him to his feet. Then we steered him over to a leather chair by the window and he sank down into it. "Whew." I wiped the sweat from my brow. Burt wasn't exactly dead weight, but close to it.

"Thanks," he said as he leaned his head back and closed his eyes. "I get breathless if I'm overly excited."

Betty rooted in her purse. "Here's your nitroglycerin tablets." She handed him a pill.

He placed it under his tongue leaned his head back again.

"Okay, what's going on?" I demanded.

"Well . . . it's sort of a long story." She began to wring her hands.

"I'm all ears." I sat down in another chair, avoiding looking at the desk area where I found Hillman's body.

"It all started four years ago when we attended a writer's conference in Albuquerque. We were in one of Jack's workshops where we had to bring a short story to be critiqued. He praised our fiction a lot and even gave us some editing suggestions. But afterward, he said he couldn't find the story."

"And do you believe it was our only copy?" Burt murmured. He still had his head back, but his normal color was coming back.

"Yes, stupid, I know. But who would've thought that a famous writer like him would steal our story?" Betty said.

"Are you saying he plagiarized your story?" I asked, my mouth dropping open.

She nodded. "I know. It's hard to believe. But he did. We saw it published in *Tales of the Southwest* last year. Oh, he'd made a couple of minor editing changes, but it was essentially our story."

"That's when we decided to come to his Writers' Institute on Coral Island and see if we could get him to admit the theft." Burt straightened in the chair. "But before we could confront him, someone killed him."

"It was terrible timing," Betty chimed in.

"To say the least," I agreed.

"Anyway, we waited until the murder had been arrested, then we came over here to find proof—and we did." Betty held up a gradebook. "Jack had recorded the title of our story with our names and the date of the workshop next to it."

"Thank goodness he kept such good files," Burt said.

Betty moved to her husband's side and placed a hand on his shoulder. "We can now expose his plagiarism."

"I still don't understand why he did it—" Burt began.

"Writer's block," I pronounced. "I found out when I was doing research for my article. He hasn't written a book in five years—since *Men on Death Row*."

Amazement passed across their faces, then realization. "Of course," Burt said, "And that's about the time he started the workshops and institutes. He's probably been ripping off people's stories and publishing them as his own. I hate to speak ill of the dead, but he was a two-faced, lying creep." He shook one, semi-limp fist in the air.

"Do George and Chrissy know about all of this?" I asked.

"No. We didn't think they'd believe us. Both of them idolize Hillman." Betty stroked the back of Burt's head.

"They don't need to know." I rose to my feet. "I'm going over to the Starfish Lodge right now. Are you coming?"

"We might swing by the island clinic and have the doctor check Burt's heart—just to play it safe," Betty said. When Burt started to protest, she held up a hand. "Be sensible, sweetie. We need to make sure you're okay."

He gave a reluctant nod, then looked at me. "Are you going to tell that police detective you saw us here?"

"Not as long as you don't tell him you saw me here."

"Thanks." Betty sighed in relief. "We're eternally grateful."

"Just make sure you get publishing credit for that story of yours." I shook hands with them and left. I probably should've called Detective Billie, but what would that do? Burt and Betty hadn't technically broken the law— just crossed the yellow tape. They only wanted justice, and that's what they'd got.

Poor Hillman. Another black mark would be next to his name when the plagiarism scandal hit the publishing circles.

I got back into Rusty and drove the rest of the way to the Starfish Lodge. My list of suspects was shrinking— back to Everett and the remaining members of the Writers' Institute. But there had to be more. I was missing something.

When I arrived, I spied Chrissy and George at the usual table. The dining room was deserted. It wasn't quite time yet for the early bird two-for-one prime rib specials that attracted every islander over the age of sixty.

"Hi," Chrissy said as she waved me over.

"Hi, yourself." I pulled up a chair across from her and George. "I saw Burt and Betty on my way here—they'll probably be along . . . sometime soon."

"Incredible news about Pete Cresswell's arrest, huh?" George asked without a trace of a stutter. His hair was neatly trimmed, his face revealed. Not bad. Clear, olive skin and small, regular features. He appeared transformed from the shy, repressed man I'd met a week ago. "I heard you were there when he was arrested."

"Yes." I noted that Chrissy held George's hand.

"Just imagine. They think that guy killed Jack because of jealousy." She shook her head. "It doesn't seem like much of a motive—especially since Jack wasn't fooling around with the guy's wife anymore—"

"If he ever did," I hastened to add. Then, I took a deep breath and posed the sixty thousand dollar question: "Do you really think Pete killed Hillman?"

Chrissy frowned. "I'm not sure."

George glanced at her, his eyes widening in surprise.

"Sorry," she shrugged, directing a rueful smile at George. "But I think Jack was up to something else—"

"Whadaya mean?" The words rushed out of my mouth, cutting her off.

"I remembered . . . something this morning."

"What?" I almost yelled out.

Chrissy caught and held my gaze. "When we were in the hottub the day Jack died, I heard him on the cell phone talking to . . . this man . . . Dr. Emmit from Gainesville. He's some kind of expert on historical things. After the call, Jack was elated."

My pulse quickened. "You're sure?"

"Absolutely. I think he was trying to sell some kind of . . . antique things from the mound behind his house."

"Yes!" I pounded the table; it was time to trust them with the truth since I now knew enough to rule out each one as a suspect. I filled them in on my theory of the priceless Caloosa artifacts. "I think someone found out and killed him so he could dig on the mound and sell the artifacts himself."

"Everett Jacobs?" Chrissy's words tumbled out.

I shrugged. "He's one possibility."

"That might explain why Jack and he argued so much about the boundary line between their properties. The old coot was probably trying to get full ownership of the mound," she added, eagerness building in her voice. "But . . . this is all just a theory."

"If only we knew Dr. Emmit's number," George said.

"Wait—I do." Chrissy reached into her purse and pulled out a pink cell phone. "Jack used *my* phone to call him from the hot tub that day."

"Ohmygosh," I exclaimed. "Does it store the numbers by date and time?"

"You betcha." She pressed a few buttons and scrolled through the call log. "Here it is!"

I grabbed the phone from her and dialed the number. "It's ringing!"

A man answered. "This is Dr. Emmit."

I blinked and tried to gather my wits. "Hello, my name is Mallie Monroe and I . . . uh . . . work for the *Coral Island Observer.* I was doing a story on Jack Hillman—"

"I was very sorry to hear about his death," he interrupted, regret in his voice.

"Yes, it was tragic. But I was doing some research on him and learned that he might have found some Caloosa artifacts in the shell mound behind his house. Can you verify that?"

"Only second hand. He said he'd found a couple of necklaces, a medallion, a knife—"

"A what?"

"A knife. He described it as very decorative, with a gold handle. Probably used for sacrifices. The Caloosa practiced human sacrifice, you know—"

"Yes, I'd read that," I cut in with some impatience. "Do you know what happened to those items?"

"I'm afraid not. Unfortunately, I never had the chance to authenticate them. I told him to be careful, that these artifacts were very valuable."

"I think he knew that." I tried to keep the sarcasm out of my voice.

"Yes, Mr. Hillman had a keen appreciation for the past."

"Very keen." My heartbeat skyrocketed with

excitement. Proof—sort of. Hillman *must* have found Caloosa artifacts on his property. "Thanks for your time, Dr. Emmit. I may call you back for further information."

"Certainly."

I clicked off the cell phone.

"What did he say?" Chrissy's eyes kindled with enthusiasm.

"Jack apparently found Caloosa artifacts, but Dr. Emmit never actually saw them."

"Unb . . . b . . . believable," George managed to get out, the stutter making a reappearance. I could hardly blame him.

"My bet is that's why he was murdered."

"You're s . . . s . . . so right," he continued—sort of.

"The killer knew what the artifacts were worth and he wanted to cash in on them himself." I jumped to my feet, trying to ignore the fact that all this news caused George's stutter to reappear. "I'm going over there right now—"

"Mallie, maybe you should wait. Talk to Detective Billie and see what he says." Chrissy reached a cautioning hand toward me.

"It won't do any good. He's convinced that Pete murdered Hillman and, unless I can find real evidence—one of those gold artifacts—to prove the contrary, he's not going to listen to me."

"B . . . b . . . but if you tell him all of this he has to," George interjected.

"I'll tell him—after I have evidence. It won't take long."

"At least take my cell." Chrissy handed me her pink phone. "If anything happens, use it."

"Thanks." I grabbed the phone and shoved it in my canvas bag.

I jumped into Rusty and set out for the Mounds. It was turning overcast again with a few trailing remnants of the tropical storm, but no rain yet. Hooray. I wanted to hike to the dig at the top of The Mounds, and it would be easier if I didn't find myself sinking up to my neck in the soft shell and sand.

I accelerated, pushing Rusty to speeds that he hadn't reached in years. And he didn't let me down. Somehow, we made it to the Mounds in less than fifteen minutes.

I pulled into Hillman's driveway and looked around. Burt and Betty's Cadillac was gone. No one else was there. Perfect. I slid out of my truck and started up the path between Hillman's and Everett's house. The sand and shell walkway squished under my sandals, but I kept moving. About halfway up, the skies opened up again. Not the driving rain of the last two days—just a steady mist.

I gritted my teeth and focused on getting to the top of the mound. Unfortunately, debris from the heavy rains littered the path. Thorny prickly pear branches scraped against my jeans and sea grape clustered around my feet. But I stepped around these obstacles as best I could.

My breath started to come in short, staccato gasps. My calf muscles burned.

"When all of this is over, I'm hitting the island gym," I said aloud when I finally reached the top. Leaning down, hands on my knees, I took in a couple of labored breaths. My legs trembled slightly—not with fear, but overexertion. I kept taking in deep breaths. Eventually, I could straighten again and survey the area.

I stood in front of the archaeological dig. Nothing much looked different, except the bottom of the pit was filled with about two feet of water, and the ropes that squared off the excavation site sagged to the ground in a couple of places. I scanned around the walls of the dig held up by a mesh-like grid. No gold beads peeped through, no gold-hilted knife stuck out. I didn't even see any pottery pieces.

What did I expect?

In my haste to get here, I hadn't actually figured out what kind of evidence I expected to find.

So I was still going off half cocked. I couldn't change overnight. In frustration, I toed a broken shell and kicked it into the pit. There had to be something here to indicate that Hillman had found valuable artifacts. I just had to find it.

I circled the dig. Then began to poke around in the saw palmetto and pine trees that ringed the site. Nothing but a fast-food bag and two empty styrofoam containers. I sighed. That and a dollar wouldn't get me into the Cinderella's Castle at the Magic Kingdom.

The mist turned into a light steady rain, soaking my white cotton shirt.

I hunched my shoulders in defeat. All I'd get from my mad dash here was a wet shirt and sand-encrusted sandals. *Great. Just great.*

Turning back to the dig, I scanned it one more time. Then I kicked another shell off into the saw palmetto. It didn't strike the ground immediately. More like, it fell a few feet and then hit water. I froze. After a few seconds, I slowly moved in the direction of where I'd kicked the shell.

I parted the saw palmetto and stepped through it. Just a few feet away was a second pit. Smaller than the other one, it wasn't roped off and didn't have a neat, square shape. The driving rains must've caused the sand and crushed shells to wash away because one side was completely caved in. The others jagged and uneven. But it was still clearly an excavation. And something gold stuck out of the crumbled side.

My hand shook as I reached for it. My fingers closed around the object as if it were as delicate as feather. Once I had it in my palm, I stepped back and slowly opened my fingers.

A gold medallion. I closed my eyes briefly. I had the proof I was seeking. Rubbing my thumb over the small rectangular artifact, I studied the design. A circle that resembled an eye was etched on the top, with crosslike lines radiating from the center. Two smaller circles decorated the bottom half, a horizontal line beneath them, and three upturned U-shaped lines even lower. What was it supposed to be?

"It's the Tree of Life," a masculine voice said from behind.

I turned around. Bradley Johnson stood before me in a hooded yellow rain jacket and rain-stained silk trousers. His glasses fogged, his features drawn in discomfort against the rain.

"You've seen it?" I asked. What was he doing here?

"Seen it? I've found three similar ones already." He held out a hand.

I hesitated, blinking with growing alarm. *Uh-oh.*

He snatched it from me. "See, the top circle is the sun, the bottom circles raindrops, and the lines underneath represent roots. The Caloosa worshipped the sun, but they understood the rain also nourished life. Both were necessary for the seed to grow into a tree."

"How . . . do you know all of this?" I stammered.

"Because you stupid fool, I'm the one who's been selling these artifacts." His tone was congenial, friendly even—in spite of the insult. "And I'm the one who murdered Hillman."

Chapter Thirteen

Y ou . . . you're the killer?" I blurted out as my body tensed in shock.

"Of course." Bradley let out a long, low laugh of contempt. "Did you think it was Everett?"

"I did at first, but then I wasn't sure." I kicked myself mentally. "After I realized you were mistaken about the Caloosa gold, I grew even more skeptical."

"Smart girl. That old man was my best cover. As long as he kept ranting at Hillman, nobody—including you— noticed what I was doing." He settled into an amused smirk. "But you were getting closer, and you're tena-cious, I'll give you that, Ms. Monroe. I tried everything to throw you off the trail. The dead bird—"

"No." *Get a grip,* I told myself. *As long as he's talking, he can't hurt me.*

207

"Yes. I thought it would scare you, but you kept poking your sunburned nose into places where it didn't belong."

I touched my nose defensively. "So I'm a little sun sensitive."

"It's most unattractive." He tossed me a dismissive glance. "Anyway, since you wouldn't give up, I decided to enlist your services to help me frame Pete." His smirk widened into a sly smile.

"*You* put that note on my truck to talk to Nora?"

He nodded. "I figured it would keep you tied up for awhile. Then, I stole Pete's fishing knife and threw it into Hillman's yard, knowing the police would find it. It was all working so well. But then you came into the museum and I got worried. So I slashed your tires to teach you a lesson."

"I was trying to do my job—writing my news story." I eased my sweaty hands down to my thighs, glancing around the dig for something I could use as a weapon. Nothing presented itself, aside from a few broken shells and pine needles. *They'd be a big help.* "Besides, I had to know what happened."

His brows rose in two delicate arches above his glasses. "You want to know the truth? It's not very exciting. Jack and I were selling artifacts together and making a lot of money. He dug up the items, I'd get them authenticated and find a buyer. It was really very simple."

"But I thought you revered history—especially the Caloosa," I said, shifting my weight to my heels so I could start backing up. Unfortunately, my feet didn't want to move.

"I do, but I revere money even more. I'm afraid that I have very expensive tastes—and a love of gambling."

Cripes. I suddenly thought back to the Corvette in the museum parking lot. I should've known better than to ignore my vehicular psychology. It never failed me.

"It all started three years ago when Jack found a gold beaded necklace. He brought it to the Island Museum and I told him how much I thought it was worth. I could see the greed in his eyes."

"He was having financial trouble."

"I know."

"So you decided to capitalize on it for your own gain." I started inching away from him.

"I had some pressing debts of my own in Miami—and those people don't take no for an answer."

"Oh."

"Sadly, Jack decided to cut me out of the action completely. He got careless. Started arguing with Everett about full ownership of the mound. I knew that was so he could expand the dig. Then one of my buyers called me and said Jack had tried to contact him directly." He shook his head. "Things were breaking down, and I had to do something. I came over to try to talk some sense into him and keep me in the loop, so I could continue to sell the artifacts discretely. But he wouldn't listen. He taunted me, waved a Caloosa knife in my face, telling me that I'd never see a dime after he sold it."

"And you stabbed him with it." I had eased away almost a foot by now, and was gauging how fast I could make it to the path. Considering my muscles were clenched as tight as a drum, it wouldn't be too speedy.

"I didn't mean to. It caused me much distress." He wiped the moisture from his face and pushed his glasses up on his nose. The rain had let up again and was only lightly misting. "But seeing that gold hilt on the knife incensed me. I had to have it. I reached for it, but he wouldn't let go. We scuffled. He fell backward into the chair and somehow the knife ended up buried in his chest."

"You could go to Detective Billie. Tell him it was an accident," I said.

"Like he'd believe that."

"But—"

"Not to mention, I intend to keep trafficking in the artifacts. Jack left his part of the mound to the Henderson Research Center, and I'll see to it that the excavation never ends. There's a lot more up here and it's all mine, now." His smile widened into a ghastly grin as he leveled a gun at me. "I'm sorry, but you've only got yourself to blame."

I gasped. Panic like I'd never known before welled up in my throat. "You . . . you can't shoot me. The main murder suspect, Pete, is behind bars."

"He's made bail. Everyone will think he followed you up here and shot you. After all, you're the one who helped bring him in."

I felt as if my breath was cut off. I was running out of options.

"Move over to the pit." He gestured with the gun.

I stumbled past him and shuffled toward the open hole, frantically trying to think of something else to say that might convince him not to kill me. Nothing came to mind. Just when I needed it, my motor mouth was in permanent park.

Suddenly, I noticed a movement in the palmetto off to the side of the excavation site. Two wingtip shoes connected to two skinny legs protruded from the long, saw-shaped leaves.

Yippie. We weren't alone. "Uh . . . wait a minute. Do you really think you'll be able to sell those artifacts? Chrissy Anders knows all about them. And she's got her own blog. That means everyone on the Internet will know, and you'll have an impossible time finding buyers." I slowly circled around the other side of the pit so Bradley would have to turn away from the wing tips.

"I'll find a way."

Sirens sounded at the base of the mound, near Hillman's house. "It's the police, Bradley. They know we're up here," I exclaimed. "You need to give yourself up."

"Forget it." His mouth tightened and his left eye began to twitch. "It'll take them ten minutes to make the climb, and by then, I'll be back down the other side."

The wingtips edged closer, causing a crunching sound of shells underfoot. Bradley began to turn.

"Please, please don't kill me!" I flung out my hands, desperate to keep his attention on me.

"Shut up." He focused on me again. His shoulders tensed. *Oh my God, he was about to fire the gun.*

At that moment, Everett jumped out from the palmetto. Bradley pivoted, but not quickly enough. Everett brought his cane down on the younger man's head.

Bradley slumped to the ground—unconscious. Seizing my chance, I rounded the pit and grabbed the gun from his limp hand. "Am I glad to see you," I exclaimed as I stood up and beheld Everett's grizzled old face. "Did you call the police?"

"I sure did. When I saw your car, I knew you were up to no good," he grumbled. "All this commotion, a man can't think straight. And poor Mabel, she's going to have a nervous fit after all of this."

"You saved my life . . . thanks." I hugged him, sorry that at one time, I'd thought he was a murderer. I didn't care if he hit *me* with the cane. I was just so glad to be alive.

"All right. All right. Don't get carried away, missy." He pulled back, but I could see a tiny upturn to his mouth.

"How long were you hiding there?"

"Long enough for the rain to soak my underwear."

I let out a sound that hovered between a laugh and a sob.

"What's going on?" Detective Billie demanded as he crashed through the palmettos and came onto the scene. He took several long strides toward me, then halted.

"Bradley murdered Hillman," I said in a quivering voice as I swayed toward him. "He would've killed me, too, except for Everett."

Detective Billie raised his arms as though to embrace me, then shook his head and let them drop.

I stiffened, trying to ignore the instant's squeezing hurt inside.

"I caned him," Everett said.

"You did what?" Detective Billie's mouth dropped open.

"Caned him. And I'd do it again too." Everett held up his gnarled cane as if it were a trophy.

"This is the gun Bradley was going to use to shoot me." I produced the weapon. "Can you believe it? He'd already taken aim, but I saw Everett's wingtips in the palmettos and knew if I could create a diversion, I might have a chance. Everett made some noise, and I—"

"Talked him to death." Everett cackled.

"For goodness sake, give me the gun." Detective Billie snatched it from my unresisting fingers. "The safety latch is off." He clicked it on and then glared at me. "You realize your messing around in my investigation almost got you killed?"

"Yes." I looked down briefly at my sand-encrusted footwear. Darn, I'd ruined my favorite pair of sandals. "But I was right. I told you that Pete didn't do it."

"Did it ever occur to you that I knew that? I'd been

checking through Hillman's phone records and found he contacted Bradley and an artifacts dealer in Miami on the same day," he grated out. "I arrested Pete because I had to when the knife was found, but I let him out on bail even though it was a first degree murder charge. It was all part of my plan. Hillman had gotten sloppy in the last few weeks. Some of the dealers were talking—I was tracing down leads. I knew if I could establish that Bradley and Hillman had been selling antiquities and, Hillman was trying to cut out his partner, I'd have a solid motive for murder."

"You knew about the Caloosa artifacts?"

"Of course. If you had trusted me to do my job, I would've been able to expose Bradley on my own."

"How was I supposed to know that?" I demanded, irritation igniting inside of me like a flame. "If you'd told me all of this, we could've worked together—"

"I work alone."

"Well, that's your problem isn't it?" I folded my arms across my chest.

"No, *you're* my problem—"

"Will you two pipe down?" Everett cut in. "Just kiss her and be done with it."

Detective Billie continued to scowl at me, and I refused to budge an inch.

This was far from over.

Epilogue

Three days later.

I stood in front of my Airstream, surveying the two spanking-new, fourteen-inch radial tires in satisfaction. They looked ready to take on the world with their steel-spoked wheels and trim ring.

Finally, the tropical storm had passed and the sun blazed down with cheery brightness. Jack Hillman's murderer sat in jail. Kong seemed almost on the brink of tolerating the beach. Everything had turned out just fine.

Except one thing.

Nick Billie refused to answer any of my calls. I'd left him voice mails with long, rambling apologies, but he didn't respond. Maybe he'd eventually relent once he had time to cool down.

When donkeys fly, to quote Wanda Sue. Still, I clung to the hope and didn't press it further.

My world had changed. *I'd* changed during the last couple of weeks. I felt like part of a community for the first time in my life. Risked my life for a man I barely knew. Maybe even grown up a little in the process. This is where I belonged—for now.

Just then, the door to the magnificent RV next to me opened, and my honeymooning neighbors emerged in all the splendor of their matching gold swimsuits.

My eyes widened as I took them in. Both tall and lean, with wrinkles from head to toe, they had to be every day of seventy or more.

"Hi, I'm Ron Clark. This is my bride, Irene," the man spoke up.

"Hi, yourself," I managed to get out. "I'm Mallie."

"Sorry we've been kinda preoccupied. We just got married." Irene beamed. She flashed her wedding ring at me. "Did we miss anything over the last week?"

I didn't know where to begin.